BEACH ESCAPE

A MYSTERY THRILLER NOVELLA

D1738198

MICHAEL MERSON

Edited by Novel Nurse Editing

Cover Design by: G•S Cover Design Studio
https://www.gsstockphotography.com/

Prologue
Old Friends

The travel trailer appeared empty from the outside. It was nothing more than a dilapidated, thirty-foot rectangular mess of cracking fiberglass to most people who drove past. Its once vibrant red stripe was now a barely visible light pink. The trailer was supported by a set of rusted-through axles, and the tires had long since rotted, now sinking into the sand. The dry desert environment of Nevada was brutal to anything left forgotten under the unrelenting sun.

It was eleven o'clock in the morning, and the temperature had already reached ninety-nine degrees. Usually, nothing but the desert's inhabitants would be out in this heat, slithering or crawling across the blistering sand in search of a meal, but not today. Today was payday for Roscoe, Jay, and Willy, and they, too, were in the desert waiting for someone.

"Radio check," Roscoe said into the mic attached to his shirt.

Willy looked up and gave a thumbs-up.

Roscoe then looked at Jay, who reached down and pressed the mic key. "Loud and clear."

The trio had been friends since meeting each other when

they were assigned to the 1st Brigade, 5th Infantry Division in Vietnam during the summer of 1969. Over the past fifty-plus years, the three had been inseparable. They had been there for each other through weddings, divorces, births of their children, and most recently, their grandchildren. The three men, now in their seventies, appeared to be gentle, frail, and kind elderly gentlemen, but really, they were much more.

Roscoe, Jay, and Willy were criminals, and the three had routinely spent time in prison, sometimes alone but most of the time together. For them, the next job was always the last, and it was the big one that would set them up for life.

The desert temperature was rising by the minute, and Roscoe was growing more and more impatient while he and the other two waited. "Why don't we just get it and go?" Roscoe asked and used his handkerchief to remove the sweat from his wrinkled, bald head. Roscoe was the shortest and heaviest of the three, and the least patient.

"We have to pay what we owe," Jay answered, using his hand to block the sun from his eyes as he looked down the dirt road for any sign of the car they were expecting to arrive any minute now. Jay was the tallest of the men, a technician, and he was also the one who was the most serious.

Willy smiled at Roscoe and laughed aloud. Willy was the slickest, the coolest, the most charming, and the planner.

Roscoe squinted his eyes and looked at his old battle buddy. "What's so fucking funny?"

"You," Willy answered.

Roscoe stepped closer to his friend. "Yeah, what's so funny about me?"

"The way you're standing there reminds me of the time we were patrolling the demilitarized zone in nineteen seventy. It was hot, and you were wiping the sweat from your head when that water buffalo came running out of the jungle."

"I remember that. You fell backward into that big pile of

buffalo shit, and when you tried to stand, you slipped and fell again." Jay chuckled.

"Yeah, but then he spun around and landed on his stomach with his face in the shit," Willy said. Jay and Willy laughed uncontrollably at their friend's expense.

Roscoe turned his head to look at the two, and in a sarcastic tone, he said, "Ha, ha, very funny!"

"That's why we're laughing," Jay managed to say between laughs.

"All that's bullshit!" Roscoe protested as he threw his hands into the air.

"I think it was bullshit actually." Willy cried aloud with laughter as Jay grabbed at his stomach.

Roscoe couldn't stand it, and he joined in on the laughter. Willy put his arm around his short friend, pulled him close, and rubbed his head. "I think he had more hair then too."

"I think we all did," Roscoe said, pointing at Willy's thinning hairline.

"Probably. Now, where is this guy at?" Willy asked after he released his friend.

"He said they'd be here at eleven. Let's give him a few more minutes, and if he doesn't show, we'll go in and grab the bag and go."

"Okay," Willy replied and walked toward his rare car. The 1965 Shelby had been Willy's dream car ever since he was a kid, and fifty-six years later, he finally owned one. When he got to the car, he leaned into the window, grabbed the water bottle off the passenger seat, and took a long drink. Today was the day he and his two friends had been waiting five long years for. After this meeting, Willy had plans to pick up his daughter from work and take her back to her place to pack her stuff, and the two of them would drive out of Las Vegas once and for all. He smiled at the thought of the two of them sitting on the beach in Pensacola, Florida, watching the navy's famous

Blue Angels flying overhead on the Fourth of July. "Just a few more minutes," Willy whispered and dropped the water bottle back in through the window. He looked off into the flat desert landscape, where he saw something shiny reflect off the desert floor.

The sniper had been in the desert since the previous evening. He had been watching the three men stand around in front of the old camper trailer since they arrived in two separate cars. Now, he was reporting what he saw back to his employer.

The sniper lifted his eye away from the rifle scope. "I have them in sight at your one o'clock."

Willy opened the glove box, took out an old pair of binoculars, and peered in the direction of the reflection he had seen. After a moment of searching the landscape, he found the shooter lying behind what appeared to be a long-range rifle. He also saw someone behind a mound of dirt. Willy turned away from them both. He dropped the binoculars in the seat and walked back to the rear of his car. "Come check out this car of mine!" Willy yelled at his two friends as he opened the trunk.

Roscoe and Jay started toward their friend. "What do you want us to see now? You showed the car to us last night at dinner. And during the entire five years we spent in prison, you showed us pictures of it every day."

"I know, but there's something back here you got to see," Willy suggested with a look on his face that the other two recognized and knew well.

Jay and Roscoe knew something was up and that Willy had something to share. They moved close to him and took up a position on his left and right.

"What's up?" Jay asked as he looked at the arsenal laid out in the trunk.

Willy ran his hand over the rear bumper and pointed to the tailpipe. "The front of my car is our twelve o'clock. We got a man with a high-powered rifle on the ground three hundred

meters to our three o'clock and one or two behind a mound of dirt at eleven o'clock, but they're only about two hundred yards out," Willy explained as he continued to pretend that he was talking about the car.

"All right," Roscoe said as he and Willy knelt.

Jay reached into the trunk to prepare the guns. "I think we need to consider the plus one or two rule and plan for it."

"I agree. You got a plan?" Roscoe asked.

"The camper blocks a shooter's view from our twelve, and the road we came in on wouldn't be tactically advantageous to a sniper. Our seven o'clock to our eleven is a possibility," Willy advised.

"Jay, you see anyone in that area?" Roscoe asked as he and Willy stood.

Jay looked out in the desert, pretending to stretch, and saw the mound of dirt Willy had described. "Just the mound of dirt at the eleven, and it could be two people in desert camouflage."

"How do you want to play it?" Roscoe asked.

"All I have is right here in the trunk and a nine millimeter in my waist," Willy replied as he looked at the M249 machine gun and the AR-15 in the trunk compartment of the Shelby.

Roscoe turned and leaned against the bumper. "I got my forty-five on me."

Willy thought about it for a minute. "We'll give our guests another five minutes to get here. Roscoe, you walk to your Suburban and be ready to cover me with our guests."

"Got it."

"Jay, you stay here at the trunk, and when and if the shit goes down, you got the guy or guys at our eleven. Use that M249 and just send automatic fire at that mound you saw. When you go dry, pick up the AR-15 and cover us around the camper. Both of you stay down between the cars and the camper. Don't get caught in the open!"

"You got it."

The three veterans casually took up their positions and waited for their guests to arrive. Before long, a cloud of dust floated skyward from the dirt road as a black sedan made its way toward the three men. The car stopped about twenty feet back from the rear of Willy's car. Three men got out of the sedan. They looked around and walked toward Willy, who was now standing in front of the old camper trailer. The unknown driver remained in the car, ready to leave in a hurry.

"Willy, how the hell have you been?" the man, who had been sitting in the passenger seat, asked as he reached his hand out.

"I've been good, Hal, and you?" Willy asked as he and the man shook hands.

"I've been better. I don't like the desert heat. I'm hoping after this meeting, I can change all of that."

"You plan on retiring early and moving?" Willy asked suspiciously. The money he was paying Hal wasn't enough for the younger man to retire.

"Why not? Now let's get down to business. Where's the money? I didn't keep the three of you alive in prison for free, you know. It cost me a lot of money."

"It's in the camper."

"After you," Hal offered and gestured toward the camper door.

Willy grabbed the handle to the camper door and was about to open it when he saw one of Hal's men following along. "Why don't you wait out here? There's not a lot of room inside this old camper," Willy said. He knew the man was one of Hal's most ruthless henchmen, and he wasn't about to get inside the cramped camper with him and Hal.

"Jack will go in and get it. I'll wait here," Hal replied. "It's okay, Jack. Rob and I'll stay here. You go in and get what's ours." Hal nodded and gave him a look. The look told Jack he needed to take care of Willy after he got the money.

Jack did as his boss told him to do. He had hated protecting the "three grandpas" as they became known while they were in prison. Jack and the others had to make sure nothing happened to them if they wanted to get paid. Right now, they were about to. Willy and Jack walked inside the old trailer alone, leaving the others outside.

"Kind of hot today, isn't it?" Roscoe yelled to Hal and Rob, who appeared uncomfortable standing in the sun in their cotton pants and polo shirts.

"Fuck you, Roscoe!" Rob yelled back.

Roscoe looked at Jay and smiled. Roscoe had the knack of pissing people off and getting them off balance. Off balance was right where he wanted both the men to be.

"C'mon now, Robby, don't be like that. I thought we were friends. Don't you remember how I saved you from getting beat to hell by Big Rick in the prison yard?"

"You didn't help me with shit!"

"You're right. I actually paid Big Rick to kick the shit out of you."

Hal could see Rob was getting irritated by Roscoe. "Shut the fuck up!" he yelled back to Roscoe.

Inside the camper, Jack took about three steps in and stopped. He looked around at the broken furniture, animal tracks, and dirt. "I can't believe somewhere in here, hidden among all of this shit, is five million dollars."

"Well, there is," Willy stated.

"Where?" Jack held his arms out to his side, palms up, and twisted his upper body back and forth while looking around the shabby camper.

Willy smiled and started down the small hallway. "In the bathroom shower."

Jack pulled his gun out from behind his back and pointed it at Willy. "Stop!"

Willy turned around and saw the gun in Jack's hand. He

slowly raised his hands into the air. "This is how you guys do business?" Willy asked in a loud tone.

"Keep your voice down. We have guys in the desert ready to take your two friends out if I give the order. Now slowly go into the bathroom and get the money."

Willy walked into the tiny bathroom while Jack kept his gun on him. Willy bent down and unlatched a secret lever, releasing the shower pan from the floor. He lifted the pan and used an old plunger to prop the pan against the back wall. In the hidden compartment were two bags covered in dust.

"You need help getting that out? I mean, you being old and feeble and all, they may be too heavy. After all, it should all weigh just over two hundred pounds. The casino you guys robbed over five years ago got everything back, except for ten million dollars in one-hundred-dollar bills."

Willy glared at the younger man. "I think I can manage it, and it was only five million that they didn't get back. The casino inflated the number to ten million so they could collect more from the insurance company."

"So you say."

"Yeah, I say, because that's what they did."

Jack shook his head and grinned. "Hold on, why don't you go ahead and slowly take out that nine millimeter from your waist that I saw hidden under your shirt. Lay it on the counter by the sink," Jack ordered while motioning toward the filthy sink with his gun.

Willy did as he was told. He started to reach into the hidden compartment for the bags but saw the most venomous rattlesnake in all of Nevada. With its olive-green color and its diamond-shaped blotches along its back, the Mojave green slithered into the corner of the hidden compartment, away from the money bags. Willy was surprised by the three-foot serpent, but he didn't jump or step back. Instead, he got an idea.

"What are you waiting for? Pull it out and give it to me," Jack ordered.

"What's taking so long in there?" Hal yelled from outside.

Jack looked out the dust-covered side window of the camper. "We'll be out in a second."

Willy saw his opportunity, and he took it. The elderly man grabbed the deadly snake behind its head, pulled it out, and tossed it at Jack. The snake landed right on the man's gun arm. Jack was startled, to say the least, and he desperately tried to move away from the snake. Suddenly, the snake struck forward and caught Jack in the cheek. He dropped his gun and grabbed the snake with both hands, but it was no use. The venom was already coursing through the man's body. Jack tried to scream, but nothing came out.

Willy grabbed his gun off the counter, then picked Jack's gun up from the floor and slid it into the small of his back. He then returned to the bathroom and lifted the bags out of the compartment. Willy heard the others talking outside. As he carefully stepped over Jack's convulsing body, he made his way to the door and stood there, out of sight. Willy didn't know what to do next. His plan ended after he'd grabbed the rattlesnake and tossed it onto Jack.

"C'mon, what's taking so long?" Hal yelled.

Willy stood there for a moment more. "To hell with it!" The Vietnam veteran dropped the money bags on the floor, pulled Jack's gun from his waist, and rushed out of the trailer firing the two pistols at Hal and Rob.

Jay and Roscoe quickly grabbed their weapons and did exactly as the three men had planned.

The sniper in the distance looked through his scope for a target. Roscoe covered Willy as Jay dropped to the ground behind the Shelby with the M249 in front of him. He sprayed the mound of dirt in the distance, and the two men hiding behind it ducked for cover.

The battle lasted for more than ten minutes. Nearby, hikers telephoned the police and watched the gunfight from a distance. When the police finally arrived, they found three bodies and a few blood trails that led to tire impressions in the sand. The tire impressions came from three different vehicles. They also found numerous empty casings lying on the ground from different types of guns.

After a month-long investigation, there were no leads. Then some teenagers riding their motorcycles along an old dirt road came across a burned-out Suburban parked next to a dry creek bed. Inside the charred Suburban were the remains of three unidentifiable bodies and what was left of an AR-15, an M249, and three pistols. Next to the Suburban were some emptied out suitcases and personal papers belonging to three elderly men who had recently been released from prison.

MICHAEL MERSON

CHAPTER 1
SHELBY

The diner just outside of Las Vegas was busy with people either driving into or leaving Sin City. Shelby, a beautiful woman with long blonde hair, hustled from one table to the next, delivering food and taking orders. It was four o'clock in the afternoon, and she was exhausted from working three doubles over the past three days.

Her boss, Frank, walked around the diner, ordering his employees around. Frank was in his forties, overweight, and a pervert. Shelby and the other waitresses had found him spying on them in the bathroom on more than one occasion. If Frank wasn't making comments about the girls' figures, he was putting himself in a position to rub his body against theirs or cop a feel when they walked by him carrying a heavy tray full of food for a table.

Shelby had been waitressing at the diner for six months, while her boyfriend, Carter, worked on his golf game. Carter had gone to college on a golf scholarship. For the past five years, he had been trying to make it onto the pro tour. Being the supporting girlfriend she was, Shelby worked two jobs at a time, hoping one day Carter would soon be taking care of her with the millions he was earning as a professional golfer. She was thirty-five years old, had never married or had kids, and had fallen in love more times than she could count.

"You need to pick it up, and you need to smile more!" Frank ordered when Shelby walked up to the counter to check for her customer's food.

She stared at the man for a moment and smiled sarcastically. "I'll make sure I do exactly that, Mr. Frankie!" Shelby replied in her Southern accent. The accent and her sarcasm were attributed to her short time spent in the South as a child.

"Look, redneck, you better shape up, or I'll send you out on your cute ass," Frank threatened.

Shelby glared at the man and then stood on her tiptoes at the pickup counter to examine the cook's food for her table. She was five foot four, and having problems reaching things or seeing things at a height taller than her was something she commonly referred to as a "short girl problem." Frank, who never seemed to miss an opportunity, walked behind and squeezed her right butt cheek.

Shelby turned around and faced the nasty man. "Don't ever grab my ass again or—"

"Or what? Nothing, that's what. Your country ass needs this job just like the other girls," Frank declared.

Shelby bit her lip. She did need the job, no matter how little she thought of it or Frank. She'd rather have worked in one of the casinos, but a felony conviction on her record prevented that from ever happening. It was either the diner waitressing tables or at the strip club dancing on them, both of which Shelby had some experience doing. "Just don't do it again, Frank," Shelby stated in a more pleasant tone.

Frank smiled, then turned and walked out to the dining area where a thin, balding man in a dark suit stood, waiting for the establishment's manager. "Would you like a seat?" Frank asked politely.

"No, well, yes. Um, I'm actually here to see a Shelby Finn," the man explained.

Frank stared at the man. "Are you a cop or something?"

The man shook his head. "Oh no, I'm an attorney, you see, and I have something for Ms. Finn. Is she around?"

"Yeah, she's here. That's one of her tables over there. You can have a seat, and she'll be right out, but don't keep her long. It's our rush hour right now. I need her helping out with our paying customers," Frank explained and walked back to the kitchen.

Shelby was still looking over the food she had carefully placed on a tray. She was just about to take it out to a large group when the local news came on the TV set Frank had sitting on the counter, out of view of the customers.

"The bodies found in a burned-out Suburban recently have been identified as Roscoe Thomas Westland, Jay Trent Johnson, and William Michael Finn. The sheriff's office has confirmed the three men had extensive criminal records and had recently been released from prison," the news anchor reported.

When Shelby heard the name William Michael Finn, she nearly knocked her tray over as she rushed around the counter to see the TV screen.

"Foul play is suspected," the anchor said right before Frank walked up.

"William Michael Finn, is he some relative of yours?" Frank asked. He knew Finn was Shelby's last name.

A tear formed in the waitress's eye, but she quickly wiped it away when she heard Frank's comment. "No, not that I know of," Shelby softly answered, but it was a lie. She knew William Michael Finn all too well.

"Well, it sounds like he's a crook, so it wouldn't surprise me if you were related. By the way, you got someone in your section who wants to talk to you."

Shelby looked at her boss with a clueless expression. "Who?" she asked.

"I don't know. Just get that tray out to its table, go see the guy, and get back to work. We're shorthanded since your friend Karen called in sick again."

"I think she's having trouble with her mom. You could cut her some slack."

Frank looked at Shelby with a disgusted look on his face. "Why would I give two shits about her? Just get your ass back to work!"

"Okay," Shelby replied. She lifted the heavy tray onto her tiny shoulder and carried it out to the table. When she was finished, she rushed to the man sitting in her section.

"You need to see me?" Shelby suspiciously asked of the stranger.

The man looked the woman over for a moment. "Interesting, you look nothing like your father."

"My father, what do you have to do with him? If you know—or knew him, I should say, then you're probably just as bad as he was, and I don't have time for you," Shelby stated flatly and started to walk away.

"Wait, I'm Tanner Scott, and I'm an attorney representing your father's estate."

"Estate? What estate, and how are you here right now? I heard them report that they just identified his body along with his two cronies. My Uncle Roscoe and Jay!"

"Actually, they identified his body a few days ago, and it's just now being reported in the media. They reached out to me because I had represented your father and his two associates in various legal matters previously," Tanner explained.

"So you're a defense lawyer. You represent people at the bottom of the barrel. Now, what could my father ever leave me? He never had anything of value to begin with. Well, except for my mother, and she died fifteen years ago waiting for him to get out of prison, again."

He gestured toward the booth's seat with his left hand. "Your father had some assets that are now yours, and if you'd sit down for a few minutes, I can have you sign some documents and hand those assets over to you." He offered a friendly smile.

Shelby stood there for a moment, looking at the tall man in his dark suit. "Very well, what do I need to sign?" she asked and sat down. If the truth were told, she really didn't care about what her father had left her. In her mind, it was probably nothing more than a few trinkets from her childhood.

"Well, first off, he has a letter for you in this envelope. Second, here's a deed for the property, and third, here's a bank statement with the money he left you in the amount of four hundred fifty thousand dollars."

Shelby's eyes widened. "What?"

"Yes, for the past ten years, your father, William, Willy, Finn had invested some of his money into different real estate ventures that paid out while he was in prison."

"Oh my word! What is the deed for?"

"Your father purchased a beach house on Pensacola Beach. Here's a picture of it," Tanner said and then handed Shelby a photo of the beach house.

Shelby looked at the photo and smiled. She remembered when the photo was taken.

"It's near—"

"I know where it is," Shelby said, gazing at the old blue beach house her parents had rented for the first ten years of her life. There, she, along with her mother and father, stood posing for the photo.

"There are only two more things I need to pass on to you. One is parked right there," Tanner stated as he pointed at the 1965 Shelby sitting in the parking lot.

Shelby looked at the namesake sitting there with its

Wimbledon white paint job and blue racing stripes. "I guess he finally got it."

"Looks like it. Lastly, this is five thousand dollars in cash in this other envelope. Now, if you can sign here and write in your bank account number here, I can have the money wired to your account by tomorrow," Tanner explained, pointing at two lines on the paperwork he had brought with him. He slid the envelope with money in it toward her.

Shelby signed the document as instructed, and when she was done, Tanner gathered his belongings, thanked Shelby for her time, and walked out of the diner. Shelby didn't know what to do. She was still sitting there looking at the keys to the car in one hand and the deed in the other when Frank walked up and stood next to the table.

"Are you going back to work anytime soon?" Frank asked.

"Oh, yeah," Shelby answered. She stood and picked up the things off the table.

"Good, now get that sweet ass back to the kitchen. You got another order that's up," Frank said and looked at Shelby's backside. He smiled, and with his right hand, he slapped her butt cheek hard.

That was all it took. Shelby quickly came to the realization she no longer needed the job or Frank's constant harassment. She looked at the metal napkin dispenser sitting on the table, picked it up, and spun around, hitting Frank across the bridge of his nose. Frank dropped to the floor as his blood ran down his face onto his white shirt.

"I'll—"

"Don't even think about calling the cops. I'll sue your ass for sexual harassment, and I'll get the other girls on board with me. That man was my lawyer. You'll be flat broke and out of work faster than you could spit if you come after me." Shelby turned and walked out of the diner to the applause of the other waitresses.

When she got outside, she stood in front of the Mustang. She didn't get in it right away. She just admired it for a moment. She took out her cell phone and was about to call Carter but decided to surprise him with everything when he got home. Besides, now the two of them had enough money for her to stop working for a little while.

The powerful V8 purred as Shelby drove it down the interstate toward her apartment. She started to imagine what it would be like traveling with Carter to more golf tournaments as he tried to make the pro tour. With Shelby working and Carter playing golf or practicing at the range, the two barely had time together.

"That's all about to change," Shelby called as she pressed the gas pedal to the floor and allowed the car to run wide open.

When Shelby got to the apartment complex, she had to park in the guest parking space because Carter's car was sitting in their assigned spot. Shelby walked to Carter's car and looked at it for a second. *I guess he stayed home today*, Shelby thought and then headed upstairs to the apartment to share the day's good news.

Upon opening the front door, Shelby was surprised to find that Carter was not in the living room or kitchen. As she started down the hall, she heard Carter's voice coming from the bedroom. The door was partially open. She slowly peeked inside and saw Carter and another woman having sex on the bed.

"Yeah, baby!" Carter yelled, unaware Shelby was standing right behind him.

"Fuck me!" the woman shouted, in a voice Shelby recognized immediately.

Shelby slowly walked to the side of the bed without saying a word. When Carter saw her, he froze. He couldn't say anything. He just stared at the women he had betrayed.

"Don't stop, Carter! I'm almost there!" Karen yelled.

"What's wrong? Why'd you stop?" Karen turned around and found her best friend staring at her.

"It's not—"

"Carter, don't say it's not what it looks like. Because from where I'm standing, it looks a whole lot like you're fucking my best friend!" Shelby shouted. She then walked to the closet and took out her suitcase.

Karen covered herself with the sheets from the bed while Carter followed Shelby around the apartment, trying to get her to stop packing and talk to him.

"Shelby, please. I love you. Karen and I were just fucking. That's all it is. We wanted to tell you."

Shelby stopped and looked at the man she had worked countless doubles for, the man she had fed, clothed, and sponsored in many golf tournaments. She didn't know what to say or do, then it came to her. She saw it sitting there, and she knew what she had to do.

Carter saw the smile on Shelby's face, and he took it to mean something it wasn't. "Baby, now see, I knew you couldn't leave me. Why don't you come back into the bedroom where the three of us can discuss this?"

Shelby kept smiling at Carter as she walked to the eight-hundred-dollar driver she had just bought him. It was sitting there in his golf bag, right where she could grab it. When she pulled the expensive driver from the bag, Carter knew her smile was not one of understanding.

Shelby removed the cover from the driver's head and made her way to Carter's trophies, gripping the club tightly. "I bought this because I thought you were something special."

Carter held his hands in the air. "Shelby, calm the fuck down!"

Karen, who was still sitting on the bed, afraid to move, heard Carter's command. "Fuck," she mumbled and held the pillow over her head. She knew telling a woman to calm down was not the right thing to say in a moment like this.

Shelby reached back with the driver and brought it forward, into the trophies. The impact sent the man's memorabilia crashing against the opposite wall.

Karen pulled the pillow down from her face to her stomach and listened to the two of them once more.

"Calm down?" Shelby yelled.

Carter stepped back from the scorned woman with his eyes and veins bulging. "You're one fucking crazy bitch!"

"Oh shit, Carter," Karen mumbled and covered her head with the pillow again.

Shelby laughed aloud. "Crazy? I'll show you crazy!" she yelled. She swung the club at everything breakable and didn't stop until the driver's head snapped off. When she was done, she walked back into the bedroom, took out more of her clothes out of the closet, and stood next to the bed.

Karen thought Shelby had walked out and that she was alone. She pulled the pillow off her head but found Shelby still standing there, looking directly at her.

"I don't—"

Before Karen could finish, Shelby punched her former best friend in the face. She then walked into the living room, where Carter had begun picking up his shattered memories.

"I hope you're happy," the upset and still-naked man said. He got up and angrily walked toward Shelby.

Shelby dropped her suitcase on the floor, and when Carter was within striking distance, she stepped forward and drove her knee right into his groin. Carter fell to the floor, where he rolled around in agony. Shelby picked her suitcase back up, walked out to the Mustang, and sped out of the complex without a second thought.

Shelby didn't know where she was going, but nothing was keeping her in Las Vegas anymore. She was a free, independent woman with nothing but her future in front of her. She gripped the steering wheel tightly, took a deep breath, and looked at the picture of the old beach house that she had wedged into the sun visor.

"It's time to take care of myself and to do for me." She pressed the pedal down and headed down the highway with the sun setting behind her.

Tanner Scott waited out of sight in the parking lot of Shelby's apartment. He was surprised to see her go in and come back out so fast with her suitcase in tow. It didn't matter if she left now or later to him and the people he worked for. They just needed her in Pensacola, where they could keep an eye on her. There was too much money on the line for things to get messed up now. Tanner reached into the passenger seat and picked up his cell phone. He dialed the number on the sticky note and waited.

"It's me," Tanner said into the phone when the other man answered. "Yeah, looks like she's leaving for Pensacola now."

CHAPTER 2
BEACH BOUND

Warden Henry Baker sat in his leather executive chair inside his office at the Nevada State Prison. He was waiting impatiently for an important phone call when his secretary knocked on his door.

"Come in."

"Warden Baker, there's a man from the FBI out here to see you," Shelia announced.

Henry felt his heart race. "Um, show him in," he nervously said. He then stood too fast and was reminded of his injury. He winced in pain and then took his cell phone off his desk and placed it into his pocket right before the FBI agent walked in.

"Good afternoon, Warden Baker," Brian greeted as he walked into the office. Brian was a tall man, wearing a black polo and black slacks. The man had an air of confidence when he moved, and others noticed, including Warden Baker.

Warden Baker shook his visitor's hand. "Afternoon, Agent. What brings the FBI all the way out here?"

Brian looked at the chair in front of the warden's desk and the nameplate on the desk that read: Henry "Hal" Baker. "I have a fascinating case I'm working on, and I thought maybe you could help me with a few things. May I sit down?"

"Certainly," the warden said and gestured to the chair. He slowly eased himself in his own seat, careful of his injury.

Brian watched the warden slowly sit and couldn't help but notice the man appeared to be in pain. "Are you all right, Warden?"

"Yes, I pulled my groin playing basketball in our gym about a month ago, and it hasn't gotten better yet."

"I've heard groin injuries can take a long time to heal," Brian replied. He looked at the warden and wanted to laugh. Somehow, he couldn't imagine the short and slightly overweight warden playing basketball, or even running around on a court. Besides, Brian knew how the warden really injured himself.

"Well, I'm hoping for the best. Now, what can I do for you?"

"I imagine you've already heard about the three men who were former inmates of yours, who were found inside a torched Suburban."

The warden thought about it for a moment before saying anything. "Yes. We sent their medical records to the coroner's office as quickly as we could. You know, it came as no surprise, really. I mean, we have a lot of inmates who leave here and end up getting into trouble again. Some of them come right back here within a year or two after being released."

"Yes, I'm aware of the high recidivism rate among inmates. Some people just can't be reformed."

"No, no, they can't. Now, what would you like to know?"

"What can you tell me about Roscoe Westland, Jay Johnson, and William Finn?"

"Well, they were sentenced to eight years for robbing a casino. They did five years, they were released on parole, and then they were found in that Suburban. What else can I tell you?" Warden Baker asked, hoping he had said enough to satisfy the FBI agent.

Brian thought it was odd the warden didn't have anything else to say about his former inmates. "How was their time here? Were they a problem? Did they have friends? Associates? Anything you could tell me may help in finding out just how they came to be in that Suburban." Brian was fishing for any information; he needed to know what the warden knew about the three former inmates.

"Well, Roscoe and Jay were cellmates. Willy had a few different cellmates, but none I could say were ever close to the man. The three hung out together most of the time at dinner or in the yard. They weren't a problem, as far as I can remember."

Brian wrote everything down in his notebook. "Were they assigned to any work details, or did they hold a job in the kitchen, machine shop, or anything?" The agent looked up from his notebook. He couldn't think of much to ask about, but he knew he had to ask more questions, even if he already knew the answers, because that was what a real FBI agent would do.

"Roscoe worked in the machine shop. Jay was assigned to the kitchen, the infirmary, and the laundry. Willy worked in our community outreach program, where he helped to train animals to work with people with disabilities."

"At least they kept busy—"

"I don't really know much about the men. I can have Shelia, my secretary, get the guards who worked their cellblock scheduled over the next few days so that you can interview them if you'd like."

Brian wasn't sure how to approach the next topic, so he just put it out there. "There's only one guard I'd like to speak to, but I can't."

"Who would that be?" Warden Baker asked, even though he already knew who the guard was.

"Jack Waller. He was killed about a month ago in the desert, along with two other men who have yet to be identified."

The warden pretended to be shocked by the news. "We've been wondering what happened to Jack. He was scheduled for work but hadn't shown up for about... well, for almost a month now. Two weeks ago, we contacted the Bureau of Prisons, and the last I heard was that they were working with the local police and... I thought you guys too. Can you tell me what happened to him?"

Brian was caught off guard by the question. He should have known that Jack being killed would require involvement of the feds. "Yeah, we're looking into it. That's why I asked about it. Anyway, it looks like he got bit by a rattlesnake. In the face, of all places."

"Where—how, I mean... What or how did that happen?"

The warden was overselling his ignorance of the ordeal, and Brian knew it, even if the warden did not. "It looks like he was part of a shooting in the desert that took place near an old camper, along with two other men."

"Wow! He really wasn't that great of an employee either. I guess for some people who find themselves around criminals all day, they can't help but fall into the same lifestyle."

"So he wasn't a good guard?"

"No, as a matter of fact, I have his personal file here on my desk. Our HR department asked that I review it before we fired him for cause when and if he finally showed back up for work. I guess that won't be necessary now," Baker said and handed the folder to the man he still believed was an FBI agent.

"May I keep it?" Brian asked as he looked through the folder.

"I'll have Sheila make you a copy on your way out. I really need to get back to work, unless you have something else you need help with."

Brian stood. "I understand. You're a busy man. Thank you for your time."

"No problem. Sheila, can you make the agent a copy of CO Jack Waller's personnel file?"

Sheila walked in, took the file, and escorted the agent out of the office.

Warden Baker waited for the agent to leave before taking his cell phone out of his pocket. He scanned his call history and found Rob's number.

"Yeah."

"Look, the FBI was just here, asking questions about those three fuck-ups and Jack," Hal said into the receiver.

Rob listened to his boss and heard the nervousness in his voice. "Do they know anything?"

"Not yet, but it won't take them long to put it all together. Where's the girl?" Hal asked.

"I watched her at the diner, and you'll never guess who showed up to visit."

"Who?"

"The Tan Man came by and dropped off her old man's car."

Henry thought about what he had just been told. "Do you have Jimmy tailing her?"

"Yeah."

"Good, if he gets the chance, have him take the car."

"You know Jimmy. He'll want to take more than the car."

"Make sure he knows we need her alive. We just want the car for now."

"Anything else?" Rob asked, already knowing what Hal wanted him to do.

"Yeah, why don't you talk to Tan Man and find out what he knows."

"All right. I'm sitting outside his place now. By the way, Hal, how's the leg?"

Hal reached down and rubbed his thigh, around the area where the bullet went through. "It hurts like hell, but it'll be worth it if we get our hands on the money," Hal answered and ended the call.

Tanner Scott had returned to his small house off Eastern Avenue after transferring the money. He was tired, and his body ached. The meeting with the woman had taken a lot out of him. Now, all he wanted to do was go to his room, turn on the window AC unit, and rest for the evening. He thought about making some dinner, but his stomach had other plans. The cancer medication was taking its toll on the man's body, mind, and overall well-being. He had been warned about overexerting himself, but the meeting with the woman had needed to take place.

After filling an ice bag, Tanner shut the door to his room, turned the AC on high, lay down, and placed the ice bag on his armpit. One of Tanner's lymph nodes had been damaged from the radiation treatments, and it was swelling. The swelling, the pain, and the Nevada heat that accompanied it were unbearable at times. Next to his bed on the nightstand were numerous medication bottles and a half-empty glass of water from the previous evening. He grabbed two oxycodone pills and washed them down with the lukewarm water. Tanner had just about fallen into a deep sleep when his bedroom door burst open.

"Good evening, Tan Man," Rob said as he entered the room.

Tanner lifted his head and immediately recognized the man standing there. "Robby, how the hell are you, you dirty shit bag?" Tanner asked in a groggy voice.

Rob didn't say anything. He stepped to the bed and delivered a hard fist to the feeble man's lower jaw. The blow sent Tanner back on his pillow. Rob pulled the sick man up by his shirt and got ready to hit him again. "Who'd you meet with today and why?"

"Your old lady. She needed some lovin'. Apparently, you've

been coming up a bit short in that area," Tanner answered and laughed aloud.

Rob, being the violent man he was, hit Tanner over and over again. When Tanner finally passed out, his tormentor grabbed the glass he found on the nightstand and threw the water on his victim's face to wake him up.

As Rob waited for Tanner to come to his senses, he read the labels of the different medication bottles sitting next to the bed. "Are you dying or something?" Rob asked without a hint of remorse in his voice.

"Yeah, and I got nothing to say to you."

"No? Well, we'll see about that," Rob said threateningly and grabbed Tanner once more.

Tanner laughed again, and Rob paused. "What's so funny?"

"You're nothing. Guards like you and Jack are nothing but weak men who take advantage of people who have no way of defending themselves. You know, that's why Roscoe paid to have you beat down in the yard. By the way, I chipped in too."

Rob became angrier, and he started back at Tanner. He gripped his shirt tighter and was about to hit him again. Suddenly, Tanner gasped for air and grabbed at his chest. Rob released his grip, allowing the man to fall back onto the bed. He stood there as the cancer patient clenched his chest and then took his last breath.

Rob looked down at the dead man. "Fuck."

Brian walked out of the prison, climbed into his sporty coupe, and tossed the stolen FBI badge and forged credentials into the passenger seat. He then started the expensive car, drove out of the prison's sally port, and sped away. When he reached the highway, he took out his cell phone and called the number on the sticky note. The phone rang twice before his call was answered.

"It's me. I just left the prison… Yeah, Warden Henry 'Hal' Baker' is nervous… He's trying to cover his tracks; he created a fake personnel file for Jack… I know where the car is. It and the woman are about an hour outside of Las Vegas," Brian said, looking at the tracking app on his cell phone. "That's not what we agreed to… Yeah, I'll do it for that much… Okay, I'll keep you informed." Brian ended the call and looked at the tracking app once more. "See you soon, sweetheart."

Hal was sitting on the bed in the shady hotel room, watching the evening news as he waited for Rob to call him. The Stay and Play was on the outskirts of Henderson and far enough away from Las Vegas that he wouldn't be recognized. He felt stressed from his meeting with the FBI agent and decided he needed some female companionship. His first call was to April, a prostitute who was also a former inmate at the women's prison. When Hal had met April, he was a deputy warden at the women's prison, and she had been assigned to housekeeping. April's job brought the beautiful young woman into his office regularly, where they spent a lot of time together. For April, their relationship in prison afforded her certain benefits that other inmates didn't have. Since her release over a year ago, she had returned to her old profession but kept in contact with Hal. He had threatened to expose her to her parole officer if she didn't perform certain favors for him and his men.

April was standing at the foot of the bed, putting her clothes back on. "Are you going to tell me what happened to your leg?

"I wasn't planning on it."

"Fine, don't then. I need some money."

Hal looked up at the woman and chuckled. "Then you better get back out there and start selling."

"Asshole!" April yelled and stormed out of the room.

Hal was still watching the news when his cell phone rang. He looked at the number and answered it.

"What did you find out from Tan Man, and why did you wait so long to call me back?" he asked in an angry tone.

Rob paused before answering. He was drunk and knew Hal would be pissed off when he found out. "Tan Man is dead."

Hal sat up on the bed. "You're drunk. I can hear it in your voice. How did it happen?"

Rob took another drink before answering. "He was sick with cancer. I didn't know. I think he had a heart attack."

"Did he tell you anything?"

"No, but I looked around his place and found some documents. I don't think he forged them."

Hal stepped off the bed and limped around to the end of it. "Really, you don't think they were forged? He was a forger! It's why he was in prison! You idiot!"

"Wait, I checked some of them out. One document was a copy of a deed for a beach house in Pensacola, Florida. I checked it out. It belonged to Willy."

"What else is there?"

"He left her four hundred and fifty grand and the car," Rob said.

"Is there anything else?"

"Yeah, I went back to the diner where she worked. I spoke to her boss, who she did a number on, and I paid him a few bucks to tell me anything he knew about the man who came by to see her."

"Did he tell you anything important?"

"Not really, all he saw was that the man gave her an envelope and some keys and had her sign a document. I think it's part of the ones I found at Tanner's place," Rob explained.

"What was in the envelope?"

"He didn't know, and Tanner never mentioned it. What do you want me to do?"

Hal didn't respond right away. He thought about it all for a moment. "Get down to the beach house. I'll have Charlie meet you there, and the two of you can work something out. Maybe Charlie can get close to her and find out what's in the envelope."

"Anything else?"

"Yes, make sure Jimmy doesn't kill the woman when he goes for the car. I mean it! You better make sure he understands. Don't you guys mess this up," Hal threatened before abruptly ending the call.

Shelby drove the Mustang for nine hours straight. She stopped for gas, dinner, and gas two more times before pulling into a truck stop gas station in Albuquerque at about one thirty in the morning. She used the bathroom inside, grabbed a hotdog and soda, and returned to the Mustang she had parked between two semitrucks. Shelby was tired, and her mind had been spinning ever since she left Las Vegas. Her thoughts ran the gamut from turning the vintage car around to staying on the road and continuing to the old beach house in Pensacola.

If she went back to Las Vegas, it would be the same old thing. Carter would be coming around, trying to make up for his infidelity. Shelby being Shelby would probably forgive him because their relationship was something she was familiar with. Familiarity was Shelby's crutch in life, and she knew it. Another crutch in her life were men in general, who seemed to always be there and always seemed to use her for their benefit.

Wait. I'm not going to be used anymore. I'm taking care of myself. I don't need Las Vegas, I don't need Carter, and I don't need men telling me what to do, Shelby thought, right before she fell asleep in the driver's seat to the sound of the two idling diesel engines.

Jimmy had been following the Mustang since she left Las Vegas, and he was eager to meet the woman driving it. He was told he couldn't kill her, but he figured he could at least have some fun. Jimmy had been patient and was waiting for the right time. He thought about going after her in the car, but with her being parked so close to the two semis, he felt it was too much of a risk, especially if she fought back or screamed for help. In the end, he decided to wait quietly in the darkness of his car until she made a mistake. Then he would take her. He was experienced in this type of behavior. He knew it would be a matter of time before she made herself available. Now that she was parked and looked to be settling in for a break, he needed to find something that would help him in securing and concealing the car.

Chapter 3
Truck Stops

Shelby awoke shivering at about four o'clock in the morning. During her short nap, the New Mexico temperature had dropped significantly. She reached into the back seat for her suitcase, found one of Carter's white UNLV hoodies, and slipped it over her head. The semi-truck parked on her left had pulled out sometime during the early morning hours. A yellow rental moving truck had taken its place. She was still sleepy, but she also wanted to get moving again. She reached down and started the car.

I better use the bathroom first, Shelby thought and turned the car off again. About one hundred yards away from her was the truck stop convenience store and the bathrooms. An uneasy feeling came over her. She looked around at the dimly lit parking lot before unlocking the car and getting out.

Shelby stood next to the Mustang as a cool westerly wind blew across the parking lot. She shivered again and turned toward the convenience store. When she reached the rear corner of the moving truck, she noticed two ramps laid out behind the box truck. She stopped, peeked around the corner, and found that the cargo door was open. "What in the—"

"Come here, bitch!" Jimmy yelled. He reached down from the carbo bed of the truck and grabbed the woman by her long blonde hair.

Shelby was surprised and unprepared. With both hands, she desperately grabbed at the unknown man's hand and muscular forearm and tried to pull away, but his grip was too strong.

Shelby started to scream, but Jimmy was ready for the ambush and knew she would scream. He had a lead-filled leather sap in his right hand, and he used it. The impact of the weapon on Shelby's temple knocked her out. Her tiny body went limp. He dropped the sap on the bed of the truck and then lifted her inside. He looked around the dark parking lot, and when he was confident no one had seen anything, he pulled the door closed.

Brian left Las Vegas, and when he stopped in Flagstaff for gas, he found, to his dismay, he had a leaking radiator hose. After waiting for a new one to be delivered to the repair shop and then another hour to repair it, he was three hours behind the woman. While he waited, he constantly checked the tracking app on his phone to see if she had stopped somewhere for the night. When Brian finally got back on the road, he was tired and in need of rest, but he knew he had to keep up with the woman and the car.

When Brian was a couple of hours outside of Albuquerque, he saw the woman had stopped somewhere along the interstate. Brian believed she was either stopping for gas or getting a room. He hoped it was the latter, as he was ready to find a nice hotel to get some sleep. As he drove along the lonely road, Brian thought about his future and his past. The past was something he wished to forget but could not. It was his past and the bad decisions he had made that had taken some of his youth. Now, he was desperate to make up for lost time, but he needed money for that, and the girl and the car would do just that if things went as planned.

When Brian entered the city limits of Albuquerque, his tracking app indicated he was very close to the Mustang. He took the next exit and pulled into the parking lot of a truck stop. The red light on the app grew larger and larger, indicating the car was close, but when he surveyed the large parking lot, he didn't see the car anywhere. Brian changed the view on the app, making it bigger. As he drove through the parking lot, he stopped a few hundred feet away from where the car should have been located. Still, he didn't find anything except for one large semitruck and one yellow moving van. Brian parked his car and walked between the two trucks, where he searched the ground for the tracking locator that had been attached to the Mustang. He couldn't find it. However, he did hear music coming from inside the moving truck parked next to him. His app also indicated that the Mustang was sitting in the same spot as the truck.

The sound of jazz music was the first thing Shelby heard when she came around. She tried to sit up but found her arms had been handcuffed to the wall above her head. A gag had been tightly tied around her head and covered her mouth. She had also been blindfolded. Shelby was groggy, but she still tried to peek out from under the cloth covering her eyes.

Earlier in the evening, when Jimmy had left the woman where she was sleeping in the parking lot, he drove around the area until he found a moving truck rental company near the truck stop. He hotwired one of the cargo trucks, drove it over to the truck stop, and waited until the woman made herself available.

"You're finally awake, good," Jimmy said. He was sitting on the hood of the Mustang, smoking a cigarette. After securing the woman, he used a come-along that he had attached to the back wall to pull the car into the cargo area.

Shelby desperately pulled at her restraints to no avail. She soon realized she was no longer wearing her hoodie, and the tank top she'd worn under it had also been removed. "What are you doing?" Shelby asked with fear in her voice.

"I'm stealing your car, and well, now you and I—"

Suddenly and unexpectedly, the cargo door opened slightly.

Jimmy rushed around the car and looked at the door but didn't see anyone. "What the fuck?"

Shelby used her right shoulder to pull the gag away from her mouth and screamed.

Jimmy panicked. He ran to the back of the truck, pulled the cargo door closed, and latched it. He rushed back to his victim and was about to hit her with the leather weapon once more when someone grabbed him from behind. Shelby heard two voices and what sounded like a scuffle taking place just a few feet in front of her. Once more, she used her right shoulder and partially pulled the blindfold off her eyes. Shelby's vision was blurred. She couldn't make out either of the men, but she could tell the fight was intense. Suddenly, she saw the glare of what she thought was the blade of a knife shining in the light of the cargo truck.

Shelby pulled and tried to free herself when she heard one of the men scream in pain. She then heard her kidnapper's voice. "Now, I'm going to put it in you deep. Then I'm going to do the same to her."

"C'mon then," the other man replied confidently.

"No, no…" Shelby heard more scuffling, someone falling to the bed of the truck, and silence. She desperately tried to see what was going on, but she couldn't remove the blindfold any farther down her eyes. She sat there quietly. Then she heard the footsteps of someone moving toward her. "No, please," Shelby begged.

Without warning, someone pulled the blindfold and the gag back in place. "No, let me go, please," Shelby cried, and to her surprise, she felt her hands being unshackled. Someone lifted her up and propped her against the wall. She whimpered and passed out.

Hal was sitting in his office at the prison, looking over Rob's information concerning the property in Pensacola. The warden couldn't help but think back to when he had first spoken to Willy about the robbery in the old man's cell sometime back. Hal had worked it out for the three men to be released on parole early, as long as they agreed to pay him half the money they had been able to hide before being arrested for the casino heist. After the meeting with Willy, Hal and his crew decided to take all the three men's money and kill them after.

The day at the camper, Hal and his men never thought the three old men were capable of anything like what had gone down. The warden reached down and rubbed his leg injury, and as he did, he recalled the moment Willy came running out of the camper, firing at him and Rob. One round had found Hal's upper thigh and went straight through it. When the shooting was over, Hal had nothing but a hole in his leg, a few dead men, and some of the casino's money. After reading over Rob's information, Hal pulled up Willy's record. He was about to read through it once more for anything that could help him locate the rest of the money when there was a knock on his door. He looked up and saw Sheila opening the door.

"Mr. Baker, there are men from the FBI here to speak with you," Sheila announced.

Hal looked at her with a surprised expression. "Show them in."

The warden stood and watched as two men wearing suits walked into his office.

"Hello, Warden Baker, I'm Agent Thomas, and this is Agent Rizzo."

Warden Baker reached over his desk and shook both the men's hands. "What can I do for you fellows?"

"Warden Baker, we're here to speak to you about one of your employees, and two unidentified men," Agent Thomas answered and handed the warden a picture of a very dead Jack Waller and two other photos of the two men he had hired out of Texas.

Hal pretended to be surprised. "Yeah, what can I help you with?" He asked after taking his time to look at each photo individually.

"Do you recognize the men?" Agent Thomas asked.

Hal handed the photo of Jack to Agent Thomas. "Yes, this one is Jack Waller, but I don't recognize the other two men," Hal answered and then handed the other two photos to Agent Rizzo.

"Can you tell us where Jack Waller worked in the prison? We'll also need the names of the inmates with whom he had direct contact with during his employment here," Agent Thomas said.

"Not a problem. By the way, do you know an agent named Brian Forbes?"

The two FBI agents looked at each other and shook their heads. "I don't know anyone by that name," Agent Thomas replied.

"I don't either," Agent Rizzo answered.

"Why? Is he a friend of yours?" Agent Thomas asked.

Hal answered with a lie, now knowing he had been played. "No, I just met him in one of the casinos about a year ago, and he told me he was trying to get reassigned out here." *Who's Agent Brian Forbes?* Hal thought to himself and then sat at his desk to answer the agents' other questions.

The coolness of early morning had turned to sweltering heat from the sun shining through the Mustang's windshield. When Shelby awoke, she was sweating, and her head ached. She reached up and felt the cut in her hairline and then she recalled the horrific events that had caused it. She frantically looked around, but only found that the moving truck was gone, along with her kidnapper.

Shelby feverishly reached down to lock the door, but it was already locked. She took a deep breath, started the car, turned the air conditioner on high, and rested her head back. Finally, when she felt safe, Shelby tilted the rearview mirror to examine her head, expecting the worst. Instead, she found her head wound had been cleaned, along with her face. There were no signs that she had been kidnapped and assaulted. Her wrists were red and slightly bruised, but there was no blood anywhere on her. Her tank top had been put back on her, and the only thing missing was her hoodie. Her cell phone was in the passenger seat. She looked at the time. "Ten o'clock," she mumbled. She closed her eyes and tried to recall the events that had taken place inside the moving truck.

She remembered getting out of the car, walking toward the back of the moving truck, and everything going dark. She rubbed her head, trying to remember, but she was startled by someone knocking on the driver's side window. Shelby quickly opened her eyes and found a man standing there. She blinked over and over but saw nothing but the cigarette-smoking man.

Shelby screamed. She placed the car in drive and sped out of the parking lot.

Danny, the young truck stop attendant, watched as the frightened woman sped out of the parking lot. He was left standing there holding a cold bottle of water. He had brought the cool beverage to her after a concerned truck driver reported that a woman was sleeping inside a hot car in their parking lot. Danny shrugged it off and started back to the convenience store to clean the bathrooms. As he strolled back toward the building, he stopped and drank some of the water.

"That's good," Danny said after the cool water quenched his thirst. He then turned his attention to a group of truck drivers who had gathered at the corner of the store to look at something. He walked over and stood next to them. Off somewhere in the New Mexico desert, a large cloud of black smoke drifted to the sky. He believed it was about two miles away.

"What's on fire?" Danny asked.

One of the drivers was holding a pair of binoculars. "Looks like some type of box truck."

Danny watched the smoke fill the air until the fire department arrived. He then headed back to the bathroom to clean it. He opened the men's bathroom door and was nearly knocked down by a tall man wearing a hoodie covering his face and carrying a black bag.

"Sorry, sir," Danny stated.

The man didn't say anything back. He just walked past Danny with his head down.

Danny shrugged it off and continued into the bathroom. He started by picking up the trash on the floor and moved to the shower stalls. When he opened the last shower stall, he stepped back in shock as to the amount of blood he saw on the walls and floor.

"I'm not cleaning this!" he declared and angrily walked out of the bathroom to tell the manager.

Brian made it back to his coupe and started back down

the road, chasing after the woman in the Mustang. He had been tired before he arrived in Albuquerque, but after the incident in the box truck, he was exhausted and badly injured. He took out his cell phone and called the number from the sticky note once again.

"It's me… I had a situation… Yeah, I took care of it… I'm going to need a cutman when I stop somewhere… I don't know where. It'll be up to her… I'll call you back when I stop for the night… No, she got roughed up a bit, but she'll be okay… I got it," Brian said into the phone and ended the call.

The sign ahead informed Shelby she was about to enter the town of Amarillo. She had not stopped since leaving the truck stop except to fill up once. She still couldn't recall most of the events that had occurred inside the truck. The only thing she knew was that she was checking into a hotel this evening. Sleeping in the car was no longer an option.

"No more truck stops for me. I'm staying in a hotel tonight," Shelby whispered. When she stopped for gas, she checked her bank account and found the money left to her had been deposited and credited to her account. "I'm staying somewhere nice." She pulled into the parking lot of the Emerson Suites. The hotel was exquisite and expensive, but Shelby wanted to stay where security officers patrolled the hotel's halls and had a secured parking garage.

Brian let out a sigh of relief when he saw the Mustang turn into the Emerson Suites parking lot. He drove past the parking lot, and when he saw another hotel on the same side of the road, he turned into it and parked. Brian watched and waited until he saw her come back out of the hotel. When she drove the car in the parking garage, he drove back to the Emerson Suites and went inside and got a room as well.

Brian took a warm shower, where he examined the six-inch cut along his ribs. For the most part, the bleeding had stopped, but the wound was deep. His opponent had been a skilled knife fighter, but in the end, Brian was better. The only thing really bothering Brian was that he should have been carrying a gun and had it with him before climbing into the back of the box truck. After his shower, he walked into the suite and was about to sit on the bed when the phone rang.

"Hello."

"This is Kim at the front desk. You have a visitor, a Mr. Smith, here to see you."

"Yes, please send him up." Brian stated and then hung the phone up.

A few minutes later Brian heard someone knocking on the door. He picked up his pistol, walked over to the door, and looked out the peephole.

Standing on the other side of the door was a man wearing a suit and carrying a brown bag.

"Yeah?" Brian spoke at the door while keeping an eye on the visitor.

"Someone called for my services," the man answered and then looked down the hall in both directions.

Brian opened the door and allowed the man to enter. He then quickly shut it and latched the lock behind him. He looked at the man cautiously while holding the .45 in his hand. "Mr. Smith, I guess you're the cutman?"

"I'm a doctor, if that's what you mean."

"It is," Brian answered and showed the doctor the cut on his ribs.

The doctor bent down and examined the wound. "You should go to the hospital."

Brian shook his head in disbelief. "C'mon, man, you know I can't. That's why you're here."

"I know, but I'm still going to give you my professional opinion before I work on you," the doctor replied and pointed at the bed.

CHAPTER 4
EXTRA TOWELS

Shelby's suite was on the top floor and had a view of the city. Kim, the receptionist at the front desk, had suggested the room. Shelby thought the hotel was nice for a city like Amarillo, but it was nothing like the hotels on the strip in Las Vegas. However, it was perfect for a woman who was passing through who needed to feel safe and secure. When Shelby got to her room, she immediately latched the door and pulled on it, ensuring it was closed. The previous day's events still had her shaken, and she wasn't taking any chances of someone coming in on her during the night. Now, all she wanted to do was climb into the large tub the front desk girl had told her about when she described the room to her downstairs.

Shelby unpacked her lightly packed suitcase, and upon doing so, she realized she didn't have much to wear. In the turmoil of leaving Carter and rushing out of the apartment, she had neglected to pack underwear, shorts, shoes, or toiletries. All that was in the suitcase were two pairs of jeans and three T-shirts. Instead of stepping into a nice warm bath, she took a quick shower, changed clothes, grabbed her purse and room key, and made her way back to the hotel lobby. When the elevator doors opened, Shelby stepped out and walked to the reception desk, where Kim talked with another hotel employee.

"How's the room?" Kim asked when she saw the hotel guest walk up to the counter. Kim was an attractive woman who had just turned thirty. She was also recently divorced, and she was about to leave the hotel for the day.

Shelby looked around the lobby and then back at Kim. "The room is great. I just have a small problem."

"Oh, what's that?" Kim asked, concerned there was a problem with the suite.

"Well, I left my place in Las Vegas in a hurry, and all I packed were some jeans and T-shirts. I need to buy clothes. Can you suggest a good place to do that?"

Kim smiled; she recognized the look on Shelby's face. Kim believed that the woman was running away from someplace, someone, or something. "Wolflin Village is about two miles from here. There are a lot of shops and small boutiques there."

"I guess that's where I'll go then." Shelby felt and heard her stomach groan. "Are there any good places to eat in Wolflin Village?"

"Yes, lots. If you need a good drink, there are good places to go for that too," Kim remarked in a soft voice so the other employee wouldn't hear her.

"That's good. I think I could use a good drink." Shelby was about to walk away when she had a thought. "Kim, I don't want to make this awkward, but would you like to grab some dinner? My treat."

Kim looked at Shelby. "Well…"

"Never mind, I shouldn't have asked. I mean, you don't know me, and um, I appreciate the advice about Wolflin Village—"

"I was going to say yes. I would love to go to dinner," Kim said and walked out from behind the counter. "I just didn't want my relief to hear me."

"Then I guess it's a date. I mean, it's a deal or a… Shit, let's just go eat!" Shelby blurted.

Kim laughed. "I know what you mean. We're good, girl!"

Brian was sitting on the bed, biting his lip as the doctor stitched the wound closed. Meeting doctors in hotel rooms wasn't a new experience for Brian, but it was getting old. He knew the lifestyle he had been living only had two types of endings for most people in this business: prison or death. Neither was an appealing option for the man. For Brian, this job needed to be his last, and if everything went as planned, it would be. In a few months, he hoped he would be somewhere running his own construction company. The time had come for the felon to finally make an honest living.

"You need to be careful moving around, or you'll probably tear your stitches out," the doctor ordered.

"I'll do my best."

The medical professional moved his head from side to side, taking note of the various scars on his patient's body. "I don't know if I believe that. After looking you over, I can't imagine you ever take it easy in anything you do."

Brian looked at the man and smiled. "It's all part of the job, Doc."

"Sounds like a dangerous profession. Have you ever thought about getting into a different line of work? Maybe something legal?" the doctor asked in a pompous tone.

Brian didn't respond at first. He thought about what the man said for a few seconds. "Yeah, I have. Have you?" Brian asked in turn. He was irritated by the man he felt was judging him. A type of man who probably had everything handed to him in life. A man who was in a hotel room getting paid to treat another man who couldn't walk into a hospital for treatment.

The doctor was surprised by the man's question. "I just thought you should maybe think about doing something other than what you do now."

"Doc, do you think you know me?" Brian asked rhetorically as he stood. "You know something, you think the two of us are two very different men, don't you?"

The doctor listened as he packed his medical supplies back into his bag. "I think we are two very different men."

"How are we different?" Brian asked.

"I'm a medical professional, and you are, well, an um…"

"A criminal or felon?" Brian asked. "Was that where you were going?

"Well, yes, actually," the doctor answered with his pompous tone once more.

Brian smiled and made his way to the door. "Doc, I think you need to take a good long look and then ask yourself a few questions before you start judging other people and pointing fingers."

The doctor followed his patient to the door. "What kind of questions do you think I should be asking myself?"

"I'd start with, how do I, a man with a degree in medicine, end up patching up criminals in hotel rooms? How is it that the criminal underworld knows my phone number? How did I fuck my life up so bad, I need to practice this kind of medicine for money? You see, Doctor, we're the same. Don't go splitting hairs about what we do for money. The people who pay you for being here are also paying me for being here. They're the same, and we're the same," Brian explained. He unlocked and opened the door. "Good night, Doctor."

The doctor looked at Brian but didn't say anything. After all, he knew his patient was right, even though he couldn't bring himself to admit it or to acknowledge it. He was, in fact, a criminal too. In the end, there was no difference between the two men.

Brian locked the door and swallowed one of the oxycodone pills the doctor had left. He set his .45 on the dresser and checked the tracking app on his phone. It appeared the woman and the car were in for the night, so he turned the lights off and went to sleep.

Shelby and Kim first stopped at a Mexican restaurant inside Wolflin Village, where they had a bite to eat before heading into the mall. The two new friends then walked from one store to the next, shopping for Shelby's new wardrobe. It was the first time in her life Shelby didn't have to look for the sale racks in the store or check the price tag before she picked something up. After they finished, the women got into Kim's car, and the two started back toward the hotel.

When they got to a traffic light, Kim looked over and saw The Thirsty Bar and Grill on the corner. "How about that drink?" Kim asked and pointed at the bar.

Shelby looked at the bar and then at Kim. "Do they have a good margarita?"

"Yeah, they do," Kim answered, turning into the parking lot.

They were seated at a corner table where they had a clear view of the entire bar. The place was decorated in an old Western theme, with cowhides, horns, and ropes along walls painted in a distressed wooden pattern. The two ordered mango margaritas and a bowl of fries to share.

"How does a Vegas girl find herself in Amarillo of all places, with a fairly new cut in her hairline?" Kim asked as she pointed at the wound on Shelby's head.

Shelby bit her lip. "Well…"

Kim apologized with sincerity in her voice. "Look, I'm sorry. If you're not comfortable talking about it, I won't be offended, and I won't pry."

"No, it's just a long story. I would really like to talk to someone about it, if you want to hear about it."

Kim tilted her head to the side and grinned. "Well, I do. I guess we'll have to have a few margaritas tonight. By the way, the fries here are bottomless!"

Hal left work and was almost home. He was tired and nervous. The FBI agents had taken up most of his day, and they had asked too many questions. The warden was getting concerned that everything was falling apart. It was only a matter of time before he was associated with the three inmates, his dead guard, Jack and of course the two hired guns out of Texas, who were associates of another inmate in his prison. Then there was the hole in his leg that he couldn't explain. Finally, there was Rob and Tan Man. Hal was getting paranoid, and he allowed his mind to run wild with thoughts.

"I can't oversee everything from here. I don't think I can even stay here. What if they got DNA off the ground where I got shot? Would there still be blood on the ground? Maybe the FBI already knows I'm involved. What if they're just waiting to arrest me?" Hal asked himself as he turned into his driveway.

By the time Shelby and Kim were on their second margarita, the two knew a lot about each other. Shelby had explained how she came to be in Amarillo, how she got the cut on her head, and where she was going. Kim told her new friend about her divorce, her job, and what she was planning on doing next. Eventually, they talked about the men who had come into and out of their lives. That particular topic brought about their first shot of the evening.

"So, are men totally out of the question? I mean for a little while anyway?" Kim asked and took a drink of water.

Shelby laughed. "Are they ever totally out of the question?"

"No, I don't guess they are."

"Shit, I'd just like to find a good one," Shelby said.

"I saw one today. I mean, I don't know if he's a good one, but damn! He was fine."

"Where? Did I miss him when we were in the mall?"

"No. He wasn't at the mall. He checked in right after you."

"Really?"

"Yeah, he came in needing a room. Well, everyone who comes in needs a room. Sorry, I'm a little drunk right now. Let me focus a minute." Kim closed her eyes for a second, while Shelby waited patiently for her to start her story again. "So he walked up to the desk, and in a very sexy voice, he asked if we had a room available."

"Because that's what people need when they come into a hotel. They need a room, right?" Shelby asked and laughed.

Kim giggled and then closed her eyes again and held up one finger. "Do you want to hear about Billy… Wait, Bobby. No, maybe it was Brody… Well, shit! I can't remember his name now. Anyway, he had black hair, olive skin, beautiful blue eyes… He was yummy."

"Was he tall?" Shelby asked and bit into a fry.

"Yes, he was. Like I said, he was yummy."

Shelby thought about it for a minute. "Nope."

"What do you mean?"

"Too perfect. Something's wrong with him. How did his body look?"

"Well, he wore a T-shirt, and I could see he was tight."

Shelby shook her head from side to side as if to say no.

"What now?"

"He's got to be gay," Shelby stated.

Kim thought about it for a minute. "Maybe, he did have a

weird-looking man in a suit carrying a bag come by to see him a short time after checking in."

"See. I knew it. Gay!" Shelby declared and slapped the table with her hand.

Kim sat there a minute, drunkenly staring at the new margarita sitting in front of her. Shelby saw disappointment in her eyes.

"What's wrong?" Shelby asked.

Kim picked up her margarita and took a long drink from it. "Well, I don't care. When I think about him later, he's going to be straight."

Shelby laughed again but managed to speak. "You mean fantasize? When you fantasize about him later?"

"Whatever. When he calls the front desk in the morning needing some towels, I'll have to run them up to him," Kim explained.

Shelby laughed even more. "Is that the fantasy?" she asked between breaths. "He needs towels?"

"It's the one that seems most likely to happen," Kim answered.

The women stayed at The Thirsty Bar and Grill until after midnight. They took a rideshare back to the hotel. Kim walked Shelby to her room, where they said good night and then agreed to have lunch before Shelby left Amarillo. Kim checked into an empty room across the hall from Shelby and spent the night.

Shelby once again secured the door after tossing her bags on a chair. Her mind was spinning, along with everything else in the room. She stumbled to the bed, kicked her shoes off, and allowed her jeans to fall to the floor. She unclasped her bra and pulled it out through her sleeve. Finally, she pulled the sheets back and made herself comfortable under the covers, where she immediately fell asleep.

"No, no!" Shelby shouted and sat up in the bed. She was sweating, and her heart was racing. She desperately glanced around the room, and after she realized where she was, she dropped back onto her pillow. She checked the clock on the dresser. It was ten-thirty in the morning, and the sun was shining brightly outside. "What the hell was that dream about?" Shelby asked aloud, then her room phone rang. She looked at the phone, surprised it was ringing. She rolled onto her side, lifted the receiver, and listened for a moment.

"Hey, are you there?" Kim asked.

"Yeah, I'm here," Shelby answered in a sleepy voice.

"You still want to grab lunch in the hotel restaurant before you take off?"

"Yeah, but first, can you meet me in the hallway?" Shelby requested.

"I'm not dressed," Kim said.

"Neither am I. It'll only be for a second. I need to give you something," Shelby explained.

"Okay, I'll go there now," Kim said and hung up the phone.

Shelby jumped out of bed and ran to her bags. She shuffled through one until she found what she was looking for. She then ran to the door and cracked it open. Across the hall, she saw Kim standing behind her door.

"What is it?" Kim whispered as she looked to her left and right.

Shelby stepped out into the hallway, half-dressed, and handed Kim a summer dress she had bought when they were out shopping. Shelby then rushed back to her room before the door closed.

"What's this? Kim asked.

"It's the dress you saw yesterday. You said you liked it."

"I do, but you didn't need to buy this for me."

"I know, but you didn't need to take me out yesterday and listen to my sob story."

Kim tilted her head and smiled. "Thank you."

"You're welcome."

"I'll be ready at twelve if you want to walk down together," Kim said.

"Okay, but are there any really hot front desk guys working right now?"

Kim laughed. "No. He's ugly, so don't bother calling the front desk for more towels."

The two laughed for a few more minutes before shutting their doors to get ready. Shelby took out the clothes from her shopping bags and spread them out on the bed. "What am I going to wear?" she asked herself, then she heard her cell phone chirping. She walked to the dresser where the phone was plugged in and read the text Kim had sent.

Thanks for the dress again. By the way, the front desk receptionist may be hideous, but the detachable shower head in your bathroom has a lot of pressure. Enjoy!

The text made Shelby smile. She immediately sent back a smiley face and a water emoji.

Chapter 5
Dreams and Memories

S helby and Kim took the elevator down to the lobby and were seated near the front of the hotel's restaurant. The two made small talk about Kim's job at the hotel and Shelby's trip while waiting for their lunch. When their food arrived, they both dug in as if they had not eaten for days. Halfway through their meal, they looked up and saw each other with a mouthful of food, and they realized they had not said anything since the food arrived.

Shelby wiped her mouth. "Oh my gosh, I'm so hungry. I know we had a taco last night and some fries, but man, I didn't know I was so hungry."

"I didn't either, but it's twelve-thirty right now. We had that taco at what, six o'clock last night? The fries were somewhat filling, but it's been like eighteen hours since the last real meal and maybe twelve since we ate a fry. We're due for a meal," Kim said as she took another bite of her chicken sandwich.

"I like how you explained that. I'm going with it," Shelby stated and took a bite of her hamburger.

"How did you sleep?" Kim asked.

Shelby lifted her head and twisted her lips for a second as

she thought about her answer. "I guess it was good, but at some time, I had some weird dreams or flashes of images."

Kim had a quizzical look on her face. "So was it a dream or flashes of images?"

"I don't know if it was a dream. It's like I had experienced what I saw."

"Were they memories?"

"Maybe."

"What were they flashes of? I mean, can you describe them?" Kim asked.

"I'll try," Shelby answered and then closed her eyes. "I see myself in a bathroom mirror, and there's someone beside me, kind of like carrying me. Then I'm in a shower, I think. I can see someone wiping my face, and he keeps telling me I'm going to be all right."

Kim was drawn into the mystery. "Do you think it's the guy who kidnapped you?"

"No, but I saw him too. He's not in the bathroom; he's in the truck sitting on the hood of the Mustang smoking his cigarette, and I'm still handcuffed to the wall," Shelby said and rubbed her still-bruised wrist.

Kim looked at Shelby's hands. "I still think you need to call the police."

"No, I just want to forget about it, get to Pensacola, and start my life over. I want to forget everything that happened at the truck stop." Shelby took a deep breath. "Now, what about you? You're single now. You can go anywhere and do anything you want. From last night's conversation, if I recall correctly, you mentioned moving out of Amarillo and going back to school for nursing."

"Yeah. I have the money from the divorce, but I don't know where I want to be or where I want to go to school."

Shelby understood. She didn't know what she wanted in life either. "Well, if you make it down to Pensacola, I could use some help renovating an old beach house this summer."

"Are you keeping it or fixing it up to sell it?"

"I don't know yet. I'm going to play it by ear."

"How far are you driving today?"

"Tyler, Texas," Shelby answered and took the last bite of her hamburger.

Brian awoke a little before eleven o'clock. He showered, dressed, checked out of the hotel, and ate breakfast at the restaurant across the street. While he waited for the woman and the Mustang to leave, he looked through his phone at the various news media websites in and around the city of Albuquerque. After a few minutes of searching, he found what he was looking for.

One news outlet had reported the moving truck fire on the outskirts of the city near a popular truck stop. The only thing missing from the article was anything about the body of James Thomas Hanson. Brian had left the man's body inside the truck before he set it on fire. Brian had found the man's name on his Nevada driver's license in his wallet. He didn't know who he was or why he was after the woman and the car. However, he did assume Mr. Hanson was employed by or worked with Warden Henry "Hal" Baker.

It's only a matter of time before they locate Mr. Hanson's body, but there's not much left of him or anything in the truck to tie him to me, Brian thought. Brian didn't like killing the man, but he had no other choice. It was either Brian or Hanson. It was similar to the situation that had got Brian incarcerated the first time, for six years.

It didn't take long before Brian saw the Mustang pulling out of the parking garage with the woman behind the wheel. When she turned out of the hotel parking lot onto the main road, she looked different. He didn't know what was different, but there was something. Brian waited five more minutes before he pulled onto the main road and then onto the interstate heading east, just like the woman in the Mustang. He pondered if she would stop once more for the night or drive on through to Pensacola. Brian looked up at the cloudy skies overhead and decided she'd stop somewhere for the night. She didn't seem like the type who would drive in the rain.

Hal made his way through security and to his terminal gate. He spent the entire night in bed tossing and turning, thinking that at any moment, the FBI would burst through his door. At five o'clock in the morning, Hal couldn't take it anymore. He sat in front of his computer and bought a plane ticket. He spent the rest of the morning, before leaving for the airport, packing his things and preparing his medical leave paperwork. He then sent it to his supervisor, the deputy director of Nevada's state prison. Hal knew the deputy director would be surprised by the sudden leave of absence, but Hal didn't care. He wasn't planning on coming back to Nevada any time soon.

When Hal stepped on the plane, he felt as if a burden had been lifted. He found his seat and placed his carry-on in the bin above it. He then sat next to a large man who had already claimed the armrest to his left and right.

Rob landed in Pensacola at ten o'clock and immediately called Charlie, who he learned was already set up and ready to go when Willy's daughter arrived. Rob tried to convince Charlotte 'Charlie' Stevens that they should stay together to keep an eye on the woman, but she had other plans and thought it was best that they weren't seen together. Rob relented and rented an expensive luxury car at the airport.

He drove to Pensacola Beach to look for the old beach house Willy had left his daughter. After driving across a long bridge, he entered Gulf Breeze, where he stopped for an iced coffee. He took his drink to go, and before long, he found himself on another bridge that brought him to the island community of Pensacola Beach. The tourists were out in full force enjoying the warmth of the sun, tanning their bodies as they jogged, walked, bicycled, or skateboarded along a paved trail next to the road.

Rob followed the rental car's GPS until he found the beach house at 1417 Maldonado Drive. He slowed to get a better look and wondered why anyone would want to buy a rundown place like the one he was looking at. He pulled along the curb and got out of the car, then a woman in a tiny leopard-print bathing suit walking her dog approached him. The woman was a tall and thin brunette, whose dog seemed to be angry with her. The tiny chihuahua barked and bit at its collar while the woman forcefully dragged it along.

"Are you looking for a specific house?" she asked in an unpleasant tone.

"Well… I was looking for a place to rent. I just got here," Rob answered as he glared at the woman.

"Yeah, I thought so. You're not really dressed for the beach. You should call Clear Sky Realty Vacation Rentals. I'm sure they can help you find a place to stay," the woman said. She walked away with a suspicious glare directed at him.

Rob stood there and watched the woman walk away before getting back into the rental car. "Fucking bitch!" Rob said and then decided it was probably better to look like a vacationer than to stand out in khakis and a black polo.

On the other side of the road, in front of a two-story beach house that happened to be directly across the street from the

1417 address, was a rental sign. "Clear Sky Realty Vacation Rentals. I got it," he said.

The drive to Tyler, Texas, took Shelby about seven hours. She found a well-lit hotel, parked under one of the lights, and went inside to book a room. The hotel receptionist was nothing like Kim, so soon Shelby was missing her new friend. When she got to her room, she latched the door, unpacked her suitcase, and took a quick shower.

She peered out her window at the Mustang. The car appeared to be okay, and so did she, but she had an uneasy feeling that she was being watched. She blew it off and made her way to the bed. She took her phone out and started browsing through her social media accounts. She laughed when she came across a picture Carter had posted. He was sitting in their apartment living room in the middle of his shattered trophies. He had captioned the photo with the words *"bitch destroyed my stuff."* It looked as though he was seeking sympathy from his friends, but instead, everyone was posting comments about how he'd probably deserved it. Some people said it was about time Shelby had left him and that she was way out of his league. Shelby laughed as she read through the various comments.

At ten o'clock, she plugged her cell phone in, turned the lamp off, and lay there in the darkness, unable to sleep. She closed her eyes and tried to recall the night at the truck stop. She had so many unanswered questions.

Who was the man in the box truck who kidnapped me? Who was the other man who saved me? Was he the one who cleaned me up in the bathroom, or did I clean myself up? How did I get in my car? Why did he just leave me there? Where was the box truck when I awoke?

Brian rented a room in the same hotel as the woman. Once he locked the door, he sat on the edge of the bed and browsed the news media outlets in Albuquerque once again, and it was much easier to locate the moving truck fire. It seemed everyone, including the national news, had picked up on the story, but why wouldn't they? There was a body inside it.

Brian read the clever headlines and took the time to see if any information would indicate to him that the police had a lead to go on. Luckily for him, there were none as of yet. He then took a shower, where he allowed the cool water to run over the wound on his side. It had started feeling warm to the touch, and he believed he needed to clean it anyway. After getting out of the shower, he carefully dried the wound off, rebandaged it, and took another oxy before climbing into bed.

Hal was met at the airport by Rob, who was angry that he had to drive back into town to pick up his boss. He also didn't like the fact that Hal had come to Pensacola because he didn't think Rob and Charlie could take care of things on their own.

"Why are you here?" Rob asked as he drove back toward the beach.

Hal looked out the window, and after a moment, he looked back at Rob. "It's not that I don't think I can trust you. I just needed to get out of Las Vegas. I think the FBI is closing in on us," Hal explained.

"What are you going to do or say when you get back?"

"I'm not going back. This is it for me. Once I get my part of the money, I'm out of here, and you and Charlie should do the same."

"Have you heard from Jimmy?" Rob asked.

Hal looked at him with a concerned expression. "When I had my layover in Atlanta, I got a call from the Albuquerque Police Department," Hal said.

"And?" Rob asked, encouraging his boss to continue.

"And, they had a truck fire of some sort, and they found a body inside it. When they were going through the charred remains, they found a wallet. Inside the wallet, they found Jimmy's old department of corrections inmate identification card from when he was on parole," Hal explained.

Rob couldn't say anything. He just looked out the windshield and then back at Hal a few times.

"What? It's all closing in," Hal said. "I went ahead and rented a condo some distance from you. I'll get a car tomorrow. Here's the address we're heading to."

"What's the plan?" Rob asked.

"I don't know. I guess we wait for Willy's daughter to show up, and then we'll have Charlie get close to her. If we're needed, we'll be here. At the end of this, we'll either have a few million and we'll be wanted by the FBI, or we'll be flat broke and will still most likely be wanted by the FBI."

"So this is it?"

"This is it. I'm here to play rough if we need to."

Shelby got up early and made her way to the parking lot. She filled the car up, grabbed a breakfast sandwich from a drive-thru, and headed east toward Pensacola. While she drove, she asked herself the same questions she had gone to sleep asking. There was one more question she had added to her list.

Why would someone save me, clean me up, and just leave me like that?"

Brian saw the woman heading out of the hotel at the same time he was. He was able to stay out of sight until she had gotten into her car. He then got behind her on the interstate but stayed far behind her. When they passed through Shreveport, Brian received a phone call.

"Yeah… Good… I can do it… Yes, I can do it for that much… Is it close to her? That's a little too close, don't you think? I know… I'll stay close." Brian ended the call and placed his phone in the center console. He gasped a little when he sat back in the seat. His side was sorer this morning and driving in a car for so many hours didn't help.

The drive from Tyler took nine hours, and at around five o'clock, Shelby was cruising down Via De Luna Drive. She rolled the window down and took in the ocean air. She felt butterflies in her stomach. The closer she got to the old beach house, the more childhood memories were brought on. She saw the old restaurants and recalled a memory of each and every one. Shelby smiled when she passed the swim park on the sound side of the island. It was where she and her mother had spent many days splashing in the shallow water.

Eventually, Shelby's phone indicated she needed to turn right onto Avenida 23. After turning down the familiar road, she gazed at the beautiful beach houses built on tall piers. Most of them were less than twenty years old, and many were being used as beach rentals. When she got to Maldonado Drive, she turned right again, and before she knew it, she was pulling up to and parking in front of the old blue beach house at 1417 Maldonado Drive.

She stood next to the car and stared at the weathered structure that had been built sometime in the fifties. The beach house wasn't the oldest on the street, but it was close. At one time, all the homes on the street had been built during that era. Still, one hurricane after another took them out one by one until there were a handful left, including the old blue one that Shelby now called her own.

CHAPTER 6
OLD BLUE

After standing in front of the beach house, taking a before photo and a selfie, Shelby moved some trash from the driveway. The home needed a lot of work on the outside. She then got back into the car and parked in the driveway of her new home. It may not have looked like much, but it was hers. Shelby had never been a homeowner, and as she sat in the car, she felt a wave of emotions come over her. She took a breath and wiped her eyes; the old house had some fond memories.

She imagined an eight-year-old Shelby walking next to her mother as they returned from the convenience store on a sunny afternoon. Her mother carried a few groceries while Shelby drank a fruity slushy drink that ran down her chin and onto her bathing suit. The blue sticky beverage was all over the child, who didn't seem to mind. Shelby remembered the white shorts with a red one-piece bathing suit under them. Her flip-flops were red as well and had a seashell print.

Shelby recalled what her mother had looked like that day. She thought her mother was the most beautiful woman she had ever seen. Whitney, her mother, or Whit as her friends had called her, walked next to the young Shelby, wearing a red bathing suit top, white shorts, and white flip-flops. Her long blonde hair blew wild as winds from the Gulf swept past them.

"Let's go, Shelby," Whit said after stopping and looking back at her slow-moving eight-year-old, who was more concerned with her slushy drink than getting home.

The young Shelby ran to catch up. "I coming, Mommy."

Shelby held on to the memory for as long as she could, when suddenly there was a knock on her passenger window. She jumped and looked to her right where an elderly woman stood. Shelby got out and walked around the car, approaching the visitor.

"Hello," Shelby said as she put her hand out in a friendly manner to greet one of her new neighbors.

The elderly woman didn't reciprocate the gesture. She just pointed at the driveway. "I'm Evelyn and I live in this neighborhood. You can't park here. Beach access is farther down the main road," the elderly woman said and walked back to her place, occasionally glancing back at the young woman.

Shelby was taken aback at first. Still, Shelby smiled after realizing her new neighbor wasn't aware that she was the new owner. "No, you don't understand. I own this house," Shelby said proudly. She used her thumb to point back over her shoulder toward her new house.

"What! I thought it was going to be torn down. You keep it down over here. My husband is sick, and he needs his rest," the elderly woman ordered. She then turned around and walked away, smiling.

Shelby was surprised by the woman's comment. "No, it's not getting torn down. I'm going to fix it up. Come back in a few weeks and see it… Bye… Evelyn." Shelby watched the woman walk back across the street to her newly built beach house. Shelby turned around and looked at her own beach house. "Maybe a few months," she whispered and headed toward the front door with the keys in hand.

Rob's beach rental was immaculately decorated in a beach house theme. The living room had a coffee table made to look like a surfboard. The dining room table was made of distressed wood, and the walls around it were covered in pirate décor. The outside was painted a light green, with a white deck on the front and another on the back. The back of the beach house had a pool and a grand view of the Gulf of Mexico. The front of the home had a view of the other beach houses and the sound side of the Gulf in the distance. The best part of the view to the front was that directly across the street was the home of the woman he had been sent to keep an eye on, which was precisely what he was doing at the moment.

The living room was nicely furnished, the air conditioner was on, and Rob sat there comfortably watching Willy's daughter talk with an elderly woman. When he saw Shelby at the beach house, he thought she looked different than she did at the diner in Las Vegas. She was wearing a flattering white summer dress that whipped around when the wind blew. He turned his attention to the white Mustang she drove, and he thought about just knocking her out and taking the car. He had mentioned that plan to Hal in Las Vegas, but Hal wasn't sure the money was in the car, and he wanted the envelope too. The warden wanted to take things slow and gather as much information as possible before they made a move on the car or the girl. Rob wasn't a slow-moving type of guy; he was more into doing something now and then figuring out what to do next if things didn't work out the first time.

"I wonder what Charlie's up to," Rob said to himself after he watched Shelby walk into the beach house.

Brian made it to Pensacola Beach, but instead of following the woman to the beach house, he drove to a grocery store to pick up some supplies. He had already been texted the address of his beach rental, the combination, and the deposit confirmation for the additional funds that had been sent. When he got out of the car, he abruptly stopped as a surge of pain hit him. He flinched his body to the left, favoring the injured side of his torso.

"Fuck," he said and sat back down in his car to collect himself. After he caught his breath, he slowly eased himself out of the car, shut the door, and made his way inside.

As he grabbed a grocery cart, he noticed the other shoppers wearing their tank tops, board shorts, and flip-flops. Brian quickly concluded he appeared out of place in his jeans, boots, and T-shirt. *I'll need some new clothes to fit in*, he thought as he pushed the cart down the first aisle.

Hal found the condo to be quite comfortable. He had spent the day settling in, finding a rental car, and making a contingency plan. Now, the warden was sitting at the dining room table, logging into his laptop. He tossed back a shot of whisky and logged into the Nevada inmate database. He wanted to search for prior inmates who had left the state of Nevada and were living in or around the city of Pensacola. After about ten minutes, he found a few prospects and wrote down their names, offenses, and last known addresses.

By six o'clock, Hal had become restless. After growing tired of watching the sailboats from his balcony, he decided it was time for a bit of excitement. When he checked into the condo the day before, Hal saw a banner behind the check-in desk that advertised the monthly "Condo Conclave" in the Shipwreck Tavern next to the lobby. He wondered what type of people attended an event like that. When he stepped off the elevator, he made his way to the check-in desk once more.

"Conclave. Who came up with that?" Hal asked right before he turned and walked inside the Shipwreck Tavern to join the other condominium guests and residents.

Old Blue, the name given to the old beach house by the new owner, was almost as bad on the inside as it was on the outside. It had a small living room that greeted visitors when they walked in the front door, and behind that was a small kitchen. As Shelby moved through the house, she detected a familiar odor that hinted at something from her past. Shelby couldn't recall the scent or associate it with anything right away. However, it gave her a feeling of safety. When she walked down the hallway, more memories came rushing back. She imagined herself running down the hallway into the kitchen where her mother was preparing breakfast.

She stopped when she got to her old bedroom and looked around at the chipping pink walls. There was trash lying about, and the tile floor was cracking in places. After walking through the entire house, she took a seat in the living room on the worn sofa that sat against the wall.

In the master bedroom, she had found clean bedding, and in the bathroom was clean linen. The kitchen had a set of dishes that were all pieces of other sets. Not one glass, cup, or plate matched another. The appliances, although working, were also a hodgepodge of different brands and colors. The refrigerator made Shelby laugh because it was new, but it was pink and designed to look vintage. At the same time, the other appliances were brown and actually vintage.

After making a list of the things she needed, Shelby drove to the grocery store she had passed in Gulf Breeze. She hurried down each aisle, grabbing what she needed as well as things she didn't know she needed. It didn't take long before she was checking out and loading her purchases into her car.

She crossed the bridge back onto Pensacola Beach and detected the aroma of something delicious in the air. It reminded her she had not eaten anything since lunch, which had been nothing more than a chocolate chip cookie from a gas station at a convenience store. She looked to her left and saw a few restaurants sitting on the sound side of the island. Images of fried shrimp and grits came to mind, both of which influenced her into turning into the parking lot of one of the restaurants.

Captain John's Seafood on the Beach looked to be a popular place to eat. Shelby had to drive around twice before she found a parking space near the front. After Albuquerque, she wasn't taking chances on anyone trying to steal the Mustang. She walked inside and found the place packed with people who, like herself, were craving seafood. To say the place was busy was an understatement.

"One or two for dinner?" the hostess asked.

Shelby was slightly embarrassed that she was eating alone. Why she was embarrassed, she didn't know, but she was. "Well, I…"

The older hostess noticed the guest's apprehensiveness and interjected. "I have a seat at the bar. Follow me," she told the guest and didn't wait for her to say no.

Shelby followed the hostess who sat her at the end of the bar, away from other people. Shelby scooted herself onto the barstool while the hostess placed the menu in front of her. "The bartender's name is Stacie. She'll take care of you. She'll even run people off if you want her to," the hostess said with a smile.

Shelby gave a friendly smile back. "Thank you."

"Nothing to it. Let me know if you need anything else," the hostess said, giving the bartender a nod, and walked away.

Shelby was browsing the menu when the red-headed bartender came to her. "I'm Stacie. What would you like to drink?"

"Anything diet."

"Got it. Let me know if you have any questions about the menu," Stacie stated and walked away to get the diet soda.

Shelby was still looking over the menu when a man walked in and started to sit on the barstool next to her. "How are you doing?" the man asked.

Before Shelby could say anything, Stacie returned with the drink and put it in front of her. "She's doing just fine without you, Billy. I got your seat down here with Carl and Sam. C'mon down here and visit with them."

Billy looked at the bartender. "I want to sit right here!" Billy, who appeared to have already been drinking, proclaimed.

Stacie leaned on the bar, getting really close to her regular customer. "Billy, baby, you can go sit with your friends down there at the other end of the bar, or you can go sit at the bar at Oysters across the street. Now, if you sit with Carl and Sam, I'll buy your first drink. What would you like to do?"

Billy looked at Shelby and then back at Stacie. "Can I come back over here later?"

"No," Stacie answered quickly.

"But you'll buy the first drink if I go down there with Carl and Sam?"

"Yes."

Billy took one last look at Shelby. He smiled at her and then walked away to sit with Carl and Sam.

Shelby looked at Stacie and then covered her face with the menu so no one could see her laughing. Stacie laughed too but quickly walked away to get Billy his first drink.

Shelby was waiting for Stacie to return to take her order when she looked around the bar and noticed an attractive man sitting alone at one of the small tables in the bar. He was tall, had dark hair, and appeared to be very fit. He wore white-and-blue board shorts and a blue T-shirt.

Stacie caught Shelby looking at the good-looking man who was sitting alone. "Have you decided on what you want? Besides him I mean?"

Shelby turned back toward Stacie, unaware she had been staring at the man until that moment. "Oh my God! Did I make it look that obvious?" Shelby asked as her face turned a little red.

"No—well, me and some of the other single women who are in here checking out good-looking men may have noticed, but he didn't. He's a man. They never notice."

"You're right about that."

Stacie picked up the menu. "What's it going to be?"

"Shrimp and grits," Shelby answered.

"Good choice. It'll be about ten minutes," Stacie said and rushed off.

Shelby couldn't help herself. She turned around to look at the man once more, and when she did, he caught her. The two locked eyes for a moment. Shelby, now embarrassed, quickly turned back around.

While waiting for her food, Shelby drank her soda and resisted every urge to turn around to see if the man was looking at her. *I just got out of a relationship*, she thought as Stacie walked over carrying her dinner.

Stacie placed the shrimp and grits in front of her guest. She reached under the counter for silverware and put it on the counter with a napkin. "Did you see Mr. Eye Candy leave?"

Shelby spun her head around and looked for the man who had caught her staring at him. After not seeing him, she looked back at Stacie. "No, how long ago did he leave?"

"I think right after I took your order. He didn't even wait for his food."

"What?"

"Yeah, he ordered the same thing you did and then *poof* he was gone. I didn't even know it until I brought the plate out from the kitchen."

Shelby listened with a stunned look on her face. "He didn't say anything?"

"Nope. Just gone. Well, he did pay for the food, and he left a nice tip. Oh, and he had a beer. He did drink that before he left," Stacie said and walked away.

Shelby shrugged it off and took her first bite of grits. When she finished her meal, she drank one more diet soda and had a taste of the banana pudding Stacie dropped off.

"Where you visiting from?" Stacie asked. She set Shelby's receipt on the counter and used a clean spoon to scoop herself out a bite of the dessert.

Shelby looked at the bartender and smiled. "I'm not visiting. I'm going to be here for a little while."

"No shit! You live on the beach?" the bartender asked and took another bite.

"I own a house on the beach," Shelby said, not knowing how to really say it for the first time.

Stacie stood and looked at Shelby with a suspicious grin. "Are you a rich girl? You don't look or act like one of those, you know…"

"I do know, and no, I'm not. It's a really old place that needs a lot of work. My father left it to me after he passed away recently."

"Oh, I'm so sorry. I didn't—"

Shelby put her hands up in front of her. "No, we weren't that close. I hadn't seen him in years before I found out he died."

"All right, I didn't want to say anything out of line, you know."

"No, I understand. So what kind of person do I look like?"

Stacie liked a challenge. She finished off the dessert, stood back, and looked Shelby over. "You look like one of us."

"Us?" Shelby asked, hoping it would persuade Stacie to explain further.

"Yeah. Us. People like me who work in places like this. Catering to others, hoping we get a decent tip."

Shelby was intrigued. "How'd you know?"

"Well, you treated me well. Something tells me that you've spent some time behind this counter or out there running from one table to another. Tell me I'm wrong."

Shelby shook her from side to side. "Nope, you're spot on. Two days ago, I was running trays out to tables in Las Vegas."

"No kidding."

"No, no kidding."

Chapter 7
I'm Shelby

Rob watched the house across the street for Willy's daughter to return, and at around midnight, he saw a small light moving around inside the old blue beach house. He turned the lights off in his place and then got down low to peer out from the bottom of the window.

"Who is that?" he asked himself.

The light and the person carrying it moved from room to room.

"Somebody's looking for something," Rob whispered and then it hit him. "Fucking Charlie!"

Shelby had spent the better part of the evening at the bar talking to Stacie and some of the other staff. She had been there for so long, Stacie had her bring in her perishable groceries so they could put them in the refrigerator for her until she left. It wasn't until after twelve when Shelby walked out of the restaurant with her groceries in tow, and the phone number of a new friend as well—a friend who planned on coming by the beach house in the next day or two.

As Shelby drove back to Old Blue, she thought about the friendly people she had met thus far on her trip. She wondered what Kim was doing. She decided she would take a picture of the Gulf tomorrow and send it to her. *Maybe Kim will come visit one day*, Shelby thought as she turned onto Maldonado Drive.

Rob was still watching the person he believed was Charlie from his window when he heard and then saw the old Mustang coming down the street. He grabbed his cell phone and tried to call Charlie. "C'mon, answer the phone," he said while Charlie's phone rang until it went to voicemail. He tossed the phone in a nearby chair and thought about what he could do.

Shelby turned into her driveway, shut the car off, and unloaded some of her groceries. She put the key into the lock only to discover that it was already unlocked. "I'm sure I locked it when I left," she said to herself as she twisted the doorknob and walked inside. The house was dark, and nothing happened when she reached for the light switch and flipped it upward.

"Damn it!" Shelby mumbled. She set the groceries down, reached into her purse, and felt around until she found her cell phone. Once the phone was in her hand, she pressed the flashlight icon, and right when the tiny bulb illuminated, she saw a masked intruder standing in front of her. She gasped as the intruder knocked her phone from her hand and grabbed her by the arm.

Shelby tried to pull away and was about to succeed when she was hit from behind. Suddenly, two people were attacking her. Shelby screamed and swung her hands and arms madly. Flashbacks of the box truck kept running through her mind. "No, stop it!" she cried.

One of the intruders released her arm, and the other intruder let her go as well.

Shelby scrambled back against the wall on her hands and knees. To her surprise, someone grabbed her, pushed her into the hallway, and stood in front of her. She couldn't see much, but of what she could make out, three silhouettes were fighting in the darkness. She heard people breathing hard and the sound of people being hit.

The third person, who appeared to be a man, the one who had pushed Shelby into the hallway, seemed to take blow after blow from the other two intruders. Still, he never wavered, no matter how many times he was hit. He kept fighting back, keeping her safe from the other two.

"What's going on over there?" the elderly woman from across the street yelled. "I've called the cops, and they're on their way." She then hurried back into the safety of her own home.

Two of the silhouettes ran out of the house. The third walked to Shelby and stood over her.

"Please don't hurt me," she begged.

"I'm not. Are you okay?" the man asked. "Here, take my hand."

Shelby felt for the man's hand, and when she found it, she held it tightly. The man lifted her off the floor.

"Who are you?" Shelby asked in a trembling voice, releasing the stranger's hand. She slowly walked to where her phone was lying on the floor and picked it up.

"I'm Brian," the man said as Shelby shined the light on his face.

Shelby moved closer for a better look as she kept the light on him. "You're the guy from the restaurant."

"Yeah, I guess I am," Brian said, using his right hand to block the light from his eyes.

"Who… I mean… What?" Shelby struggled to speak as she walked into the kitchen and turned on another light.

Brian had to come up with something fast. This wasn't

part of the plan. "I'm staying next door, and when I got home, I heard you screaming. I ran over here and found, well, all of this. Who were those people?" he asked, attempting to redirect the line of questioning.

Shelby cautiously walked back toward the handsome stranger. "Why'd you leave the restaurant in such a hurry earlier?"

The redirect didn't work. "I haven't been feeling well since I got here, and I thought I was going to get sick. I paid for my food and walked out to the beach. The next thing I know is I'm lying on the sand, and it's after midnight," Brian said as the sound of police sirens got louder and louder.

Shelby looked at Brian and placed her hand on his forehead. He was burning with fever. "Come over here and sit down," Shelby ordered, just as her rescuer passed out and fell to the floor.

When Rob got back to his place, he kept the lights off and sat on the floor, spying on the events unfolding next door. First, there were two police cars, then a third. Next came an ambulance, which carried off the man who had come in and attacked Charlie and him. He tightened his jaw and gritted his teeth when he thought about how Charlie may have ruined everything for them. He waited for the police and the ambulance to leave before he crawled into the back bedroom, where he shut the door and took out his cell phone.

He texted Charlie and then waited. *What the fuck was that about?*

I didn't need any help!

Rob read the text and gritted his teeth. *The fuck you didn't! I saved your ass.*

Whatever! Who was the guy?

I don't know. I'll see if Hal has an idea. Rob answered.
Don't interfere with me again!

Fuck you! Rob typed and then dropped the phone between his legs.

Shelby went to the hospital to be treated for some minor injuries, along with the man she knew only as Brian. One of the responding deputies followed her to the hospital and got her statement. She answered as many of the deputy's questions that she could, which wasn't many. After all, she didn't know who the other two intruders were. She never got a good look at them, nor did she know what they were after or where they had run off to. The only thing she was sure about was that Brian had come over and saved her from unknown harm. She also knew he was a mystery man whom she wanted to learn more about, and it was why she stayed at the hospital after being treated for minor scrapes and bruises.

"I'm Doctor Williams. Are you Mr. Brian Suther's next of kin?" the treating physician asked.

Shelby thought about the question for about half of a second. "Yes, he's my fiancé. Is he going to be okay?"

The doctor looked at her with a suspicious glare, and Shelby knew he was questioning what she had just said.

"I mean, I'm just so worried. We were at dinner earlier, and he said he didn't feel good, so we went out to the beach, and he passed out. I ran into the restaurant to get some help, but when I got back, he was awake. I wanted to bring him in then, but he refused—stubborn ass. Anyway, when we got back to our beach house, we were attacked. You can ask the deputy; I think he's still here." Shelby halfheartedly started to stand as if she were about to go locate the deputy.

"No, that won't be necessary," the doctor said, interjecting. Your fiancé has an infection."

"An infection?" Shelby blurted as her mind thought about specific infections.

The doctor looked at her with raised eyebrows. "Yes, like I was saying, he has an infection. Can you tell me how he got that deep cut on his left side?"

Shelby looked at Brian, who still appeared to be unconscious, and back at the doctor, not knowing what to say. "How did he get the cut on his side?" She repeated the question hoping to buy some time.

"Yes, how did it happen?"

Shelby opened her mouth but felt Brian's hand on her arm.

"Where am I?" Brian asked.

"You're in the emergency room at Baptist Hospital. You and your fiancée were brought in after you were attacked. She was just about to tell me how you got that cut on your side, that appears to be infected."

"I fell off the roof at one of my job sites. I'm a custom home builder, and right before we left for vacation, I slipped and slid over a piece of roofing flange that had a sharp edge. It cut me pretty bad. My doctor back home stitched it up," Brian said, lifting his left arm to examine the wound himself.

"Well, the stitches tore loose from whatever you two got into this evening, but the cut was infected before then. I've given you some antibiotics that should take care of it. I would like to admit you for the night for observation."

"Is it really necessary?" Brian asked.

"Well, I wouldn't have suggested it if it weren't, would I?"

Brian chuckled and looked at Shelby. "If my fiancée promises to take care of me and to watch over me, would that be good enough?"

The doctor looked at his patient and rolled his eyes. "I don't care if you stay the night or not. If you want her to watch you, then that's up to you. You will be leaving here against medical advice. I'll send you home with more antibiotics, guidelines to follow, and what to look out for regarding infections. We've covered the wound for now, but the wound itself needs to stay open for a little bit longer. In a few days, come back, and we'll close it up. Keep it clean and apply a new dressing every day."

"Okay, then that's what we'll do," Shelby answered, seeing the doctor was getting impatient with his patient.

"It'll be a few minutes. Sit tight, and someone will come back and sign you out," the good doctor stated and walked out of the room.

Brian looked at Shelby. "Fiancé?"

"I'm sorry, I didn't know what else to say. I wanted to make sure you were okay, and he wasn't going to tell me unless I was your next of kin."

"All right, I understand, but whose place are we staying at tonight?"

"Oh no, I'm staying at my place, and you're staying at yours. I'll come over and help you if you need anything. I'll give you my number, and you can call me," Shelby replied, clarifying immediately. "Oh, and you need to call this man tomorrow." Shelby handed Brian a business card.

"Who's this?"

"It's the deputy who took my report. He needs your statement."

"What about you?"

"I already gave him my statement. You were asleep."

Brian looked at Shelby while she looked out the door toward the hall. He thought she was beautiful. "What's your name?"

Shelby looked back at the half-dressed, good-looking man lying in the hospital bed who just happened to be the same man who had protected her. "I guess we haven't been formally introduced, have we?"

71

"No, we haven't. I mean, I told you who I was, but you never told me who you were."

"Well, you did pass out."

"Yeah, I guess I did."

"I'm Shelby."

Shelby and Brian took a rideshare back to the beach house and got there at about five o'clock in the morning. After they walked through her place to make sure it was safe and to get the lights back on, Brian walked back to his. When Brian walked inside, he found his cell phone right where he had left it before running over to Shelby's place earlier. He picked it up and saw he had numerous missed calls from one number. He called the number back and waited for him to answer.

"It's me... Yeah, things got bad last night. Someone made a move on her... Yeah, she's fine, and so am I. Thanks for asking... No, I don't know who it was... It was dark... I don't know... Well, I was over here, and I saw someone moving around inside her place with a flashlight as she was coming back from dinner... I went over there and found two people attacking her, so I stopped them... I don't know. They took off... Yeah, fine. I got to get some sleep," Brian said and ended the call.

He checked the locks on his doors and windows before he headed to his bedroom. When he got to his bed, he took a seat on the edge and looked at his .45 sitting on the nightstand. "That's twice now I needed you, and you weren't there for me," he said and picked the gun up. He figured the infection and the fever had clouded his thoughts, which caused him to run out of the house without the weapon. "That had to be it, right? Or was it something or someone else distracting me?"

Shelby walked into the bathroom and turned on the

shower, but nothing happened. She turned both knobs, but no water spewed from the showerhead or the faucet. She tried the hot and cold knobs on the sink, and to her delighted surprise, water rushed out. She took her clothes off, wet a washcloth, and bathed herself over a towel. "This will have to do for tonight," she mumbled.

After Shelby's birdbath, as she called it, she put on clean clothes and rechecked the front door and windows, making sure they were locked. She grabbed an empty glass bottle she had found in the yard and carefully balanced it on the front door's knob. If it were opened, the bottle would fall to the tile floor and make a loud shattering noise. It was a trick her father had taught her when she was a teenager.

When Shelby fell asleep, she was haunted by faint and broken memories from the night at the truck stop in Albuquerque. This time, she had different memories or visions.

Once again, she was in the back of the box truck. She found herself being carried by someone wearing a red-and-white hoodie that covered their head and darkened their face. Shelby felt calm and safe as the man carried her through the parking lot toward the convenience store, where the glow of the fluorescent lights blinded her. She closed her eyes and heard him whisper, "You'll be all right." She heard the bathroom door open and opened her eyes. The lights inside were just as bright. Unexpectedly and to her delight, she saw the man tilting his head down to look at her. Shelby got excited; she could almost see his face.

A chiming noise came from somewhere outside her memory, and just like that, he was gone. Shelby was lying in her bed right next to her phone, which was ringing on the dresser.

Shelby rolled over and looked at her phone. It was noon and Brian was calling. "Hello," she said in a tired but cheerful voice.

"I need some help," Brian stated.

Shelby quickly sat up. "Are you okay?"

"Yes, but can you come over here, please?" Brian asked in a quiet voice.

"I'll be right there."

Shelby dressed quickly, put her hair into a ponytail, and took one last look in the mirror. She grabbed her cell phone, unlocked the front door, and hurried to the beach house next door.

Rob was dressed and getting ready to leave to meet with Hal when he saw the woman rush to the beach house next door. "What's this about?" he asked aloud.

CHAPTER 8
LANCE AND BRENDA

The beach house is picture-perfect. Brenda typed it just like that and texted it with a picture to her daughter back in Ohio. Brenda and her husband, Lance, were in their sixties and had come to Pensacola for the summer to look for a new house to retire in. Lance had found the summer rental online and spoken to the owner. The owner informed Lance the rental unit was available and that it was being sold at the end of the summer. When Lance showed Brenda pictures of the beach house, she immediately fell in love with it. She especially loved how it was designed and built with an Italian villa theme. It was a light-brown stucco with a dark-brown clay-tile roof. The beach house had a large deck in the back with a saltwater swimming pool.

The couple had spent the first two weeks looking at other homes on Pensacola Beach, in case there was something available they liked better. Still, in the end, they decided on the one they were renting, the one Brenda had already fallen in love with. They told the owner they had decided to purchase the beach house. The owner generously agreed to allow them to stay in their future home rent-free until they closed on it during the first week of August. The couple was ecstatic about their future home, and Brenda told everyone she met on the island about it, including a stranger named Charlie.

Charlie said she was also in Pensacola looking for some property. When Lance and Brenda met Charlie, the three immediately hit it off. The couple invited their new friend back to their place for dinner. Charlie seemed excited for the soon-to-be retirees. They generously gave their visitor a tour of what was to be their new home.

The home tour ended in the garage, where the couple's brand-new luxury car was parked. They had purchased it the previous day. Charlie convinced them to get inside the car for a photo Brenda could send to their daughter.

Now, a few days later Charlie's back was sore from the burglary and the fight. When she returned from the old blue beach house, Charlie needed something to ease her lower back pain. After looking around the bathroom for some pills, she walked downstairs to the kitchen and noticed a foul odor.

Charlie looked at the door leading to the garage. It was time to check on Lance and Brenda, who were still in the garage, sitting in their car with a bullet in their heads. She opened the door and found the source of the foul odor. Lance and Brenda had gotten quite ripe. Charlie quickly shut the door and decided something needed to be done with the couple before other people in the neighborhood started smelling their decomposing bodies.

Shelby rushed into Brian's place expecting to find the man in a bad way, but instead, she found him sitting on a leather sofa with a roguish grin and watching golf of all things. Shelby stared at the man with a sullen expression.

"I thought you needed help," she said as she walked into the room.

Brian stood and took a good look at the beautiful woman who rushed over to help him. "I do. I need help eating that pizza over there. I ordered it, and when it arrived, I took one look and knew I couldn't eat it all myself," Brian said as he pointed into the dining room.

Shelby didn't respond. She walked into the dining room and looked at the pizza box and the two bottles of beer sitting in an ice bucket next to it. "Does this place have ranch dressing?" Shelby asked and sat down.

"It does. I'll be right back," Brian stated as he rushed into the kitchen.

Hal sat patiently at the picnic table, waiting for Rob. Hal had thought about what he needed to do when he got back from the Condo Conclave the previous night. After more careful deliberation, he decided to steal the car. His decision didn't come easy, but after Charlie told him nothing had been found in the beach house, there were only so many options left. If the money wasn't in the Mustang, then Willy's daughter had to know where it was. Hal figured he was down to either getting the car, the letter Tan Man delivered, or the girl. One of the three had to lead the warden to his retirement.

Rob found Hawkins Recreational Park off Munson Highway in the town of Milton. He didn't know why Hal wanted to meet this far away from Pensacola Beach, but it didn't matter. Hal was the boss, so he called the shots. When Rob pulled into the parking lot, he found Hal sitting near the river at one of the picnic tables.

"Why are we meeting out here?" Rob asked.

Hal looked at the people around them. "You carrying?"

"Yeah, why?" Rob answered as he pulled his shirt up, revealing the handle of his 9 mm.

"Good. We're meeting José Hernandez and his brother, Mateo."

Rob raised an eyebrow as he looked at his boss suspiciously. "You think we need them?"

"Maybe; Charlie called and told me there was nothing in the beach house. So either the cash is in the car or there's information in the envelope Tan Man delivered that will lead us to it."

"If there isn't?"

"Then we always have the girl."

Rob looked down at the table. "Yeah, but now she has help."

"How good is he?"

"He took on Charlie and me. He didn't seem to mind being outnumbered in a fight," Rob reluctantly said.

Hal thought about it for a moment. "Do you think he's a pro?"

"Possibly," Rob answered as two men walked over and stood next to them. Rob recognized the two men, so he moved around the table and stood behind Hal, ready to pull his gun if needed.

José and Mateo Hernandez didn't know what to expect when they got the call to meet with their former prison warden. Since they were both still on parole, they figured they had best make the meeting.

"Warden," José said and looked up at Rob.

"Fellas, how's life on the outside treating you? Contributing to the betterment of society, I hope," Hal said sarcastically.

"What's up? Why you in Florida? We ain't violating parole. We got permission to be here," José replied, while Mateo continued to keep his eyes on Rob. Mateo recognized the prison guard.

"No, you're not in violation."

"Then why you fucking with us?" Mateo asked.

Hal stood and walked closer to the two men. "I'm not. I'm here to offer the two of you a job. If I remember correctly, you guys are for hire. Correct?"

The two brothers looked at each other with a curious expression. "You want to hire us?" José asked.

"Yes."

"It's a trap. We agree to do something and then you revoke our parole."

Hal shook his head. "No, you don't do what I need, and I'll revoke it. So you have two choices here. Either you do what I need done and make some money, or you walk away and I make some phone calls to send you back," Hal stated and then dropped ten thousand dollars on the picnic table.

Shelby and Brian moved into the living room after they finished eating. They sat close to each other on the sofa. Shelby enjoyed the man's company, and it didn't hurt that he was easy on the eyes.

Brian also enjoyed looking at and talking to the woman he had saved twice.

Shelby pulled her legs under her and twisted her body to face him. "So, tell me about Brian Suthers."

"Suthers? I don't remember telling you my last name."

Shelby gave a cheeky grin. "The doctor said it before you came around last night. I also read it on your discharge papers too."

"Oh, I see."

"What do you expect? You came in when I needed help and probably saved my life. I wanted to know who you were. Now, I would like to find out more about you," Shelby explained and took a sip of her beer.

"Well, I'm Brian Suthers. I grew up in North Carolina. My

parents still live there. I joined the US Army after high school and spent some time overseas."

"What'd you do in the army?"

Brian didn't know how he should answer the question. He hesitated.

"That bad?" Shelby asked when she saw the blank look on the man's face.

"No, it's just not what some people want to hear about."

Shelby understood. She had once asked her father what he did in Vietnam, and he'd had the same look. "We don't have to talk about it. So what did you do after getting out of the army?"

Brian looked at her once again with a blank expression. Before Shelby could say anything, he blurted, "I spent six years in prison."

Shelby was in shock, and her face showed it. "Interesting."

"If you want to leave now, I understand," Brian said and moved to stand.

Shelby reached over and grabbed his arm. "No, stay here and tell me about it." There was something about Brian that drew her to him. She wanted to know everything about him.

Brian took a deep breath. "When I got back from my last deployment, I was in a different place mentally. I went out one night to a bar and drank heavily. This guy came over, and he saw my haircut. He assumed correctly that I was in the military. He wanted to buy me another drink. His name was Walt, and he was really drunk, and he had two friends with him," Brian said and then took a moment.

Shelby saw it was hard for him to share his story. "Go on. It's all right."

"Well, I was young, and I wasn't in the mood for company, but Walt wouldn't stop. I told him I wanted to be alone. Walt put his hand on my shoulder and spun me around when I tried to ignore him. I stood up and pushed him away. He came toward me again, and I wasn't having it. I grabbed a heavy beer mug and hit Walt in the head with it."

"Did you kill him?" Shelby asked.

"No, but what I didn't know was that Walt had a brain injury from a car crash he got into a few years prior to that night. The blow from the mug caused him to have a seizure that paralyzed his right side."

"You were charged."

"Yeah, first-degree assault causing bodily injury. The army discharged me, and I did six years in prison for it."

Shelby set her beer on the coffee table. "My father was in and out of prison my entire life. He was always after the big score that never seemed to pan out. When I was really young, I used my crayons and drew him a picture of us in front of the beach house. My mother sent it to him in prison, but he never wrote back or ever said anything about it."

"What about your mother?"

"Oh, always the faithful bride. She waited for him to get out of prison each and every time he was sent away. She died of pancreatic cancer when I was fifteen. I pretty much stopped going to school and took care of her."

Brian took the last drink of his beer and set his bottle next to hers. "Where was your father?"

Shelby shifted her eyes upward. "Prison, of course. She died on a Friday, and he was released the following Monday."

"Did he walk away after that?"

"No, he tried to be a father. He got a job selling tires, and he kept it the entire time I was in school."

"I thought you stopped going to school."

"I did, but after my mother died, I went back. I did everything I could to stay out of the house and away from him."

Brian gave her a questioning look. "I don't understand. Was he an abusive man?"

"No. Not at all."

"Did he drink?"

"Yeah, but he wasn't an alcoholic or anything like that," Shelby answered. The questions made her start to think. "Enough about me. Tell me more about you."

"Like what?"

"How did you adapt to prison life? Or is that too personal?"

"No, I can talk about it. It was bad at first. I didn't consider myself one of them. I saw everyone around me as a murderer or rapist. Now, don't get me wrong, I've killed people in war who were trying to kill me, so I'm not a saint, but I never killed an innocent person."

"How did you get by?"

"It was hard. If I wasn't in a fight, then I was in solitary because I had been in a fight. That went on for like six months. Then one day, I get out of solitary, and when I get to my cell block, there's this old guy in my cell."

Shelby lowered her head. "Was he a hardened criminal?"

"Criminal, yes. Career criminal actually, but not hardened by any means."

"Well, what happened?"

Brian shrugged his shoulders. "Nothing really. He wasn't a murderer or a rapist. I tried to act hard at first, but he blew it off."

Shelby raised her head. "You tried to be hard."

Brian laughed. "Yeah, I walked in and said I'm taking this or that. He didn't argue about it. I was rude to him for like two weeks straight. Then I started to notice a pattern."

"A pattern?"

"Yeah, every time I did something to this guy, I got a shitty work assignment the next day. Eventually, I learned that his old man was running the show."

"Really!"

"Yeah, he had guards on the take. He never did anything he didn't want to do. This guy got special meals, rec time, and gifts."

Shelby had a look of curiosity on her face. "Gifts."

Brian nodded. "Yeah, he got gifts from people. We had a small TV, a toaster oven, and once every month, he got us ice cream."

"Ice cream."

"Oh yes, it was vanilla ice cream that had chocolate chips and caramel mixed into it."

"You got to eat it too."

Brian leaned forward onto his knees. "Well, yeah. You see, I caught on really quick to this guy running things, so I stopped being an asshole to him. Then one day in the rec yard, this other inmate starts in on him about something and tries to stab him. For some reason, I stepped in and stopped the inmate, and from then on, I was his guy."

Shelby squinted her eyes. "His guy?"

"Yeah, I made sure nothing happened to him."

"Kind of like with me the other night, a bodyguard of sorts."

Brian shrugged his shoulders. "Yeah, I guess."

Shelby looked out the window at the Gulf of Mexico in the distance. She then looked back at her bodyguard. "I haven't walked on the beach since I've been here. You feel up to it?"

"Yeah."

The drive to the Florida-Alabama line took Charlie about an hour. An hour with two decaying bodies in the trunk was more than she had bargained for. More than once, the killer had to stop and take a break, out of the car from the stench. A dirt road off Mobile Hwy took the killer into the woods near Styx River.

Charlie drove the luxury car about three miles down the dirt road until she reached a clearing near the river's edge. Charlie parked the car and casually looked around. She wasted no time pulling Lance and Brenda out of the trunk and dragging them to the riverbank. The last thing Charlie saw of the couple was their bodies sinking deeper into the water as the current carried them away.

Charlie opened the doors and the car's trunk to let it air out before heading back to the beach. The killer then lit a cigarette and smoked it while reading the text message Hal had sent.

Meet us at Rob's beach rental at nine o'clock. We're taking the car tonight.

"Finally," Charlie mumbled. She tossed her still-lit cigarette to the ground and got ready to leave but heard someone walking out of the brush behind her. She quickly turned around and found two men dressed in camouflage.

"You lost?" one of the men asked as he approached her. Beau and his brother had been shooting birds when they came across the woman who was alone and looked helpless.

Charlie knew the type of men they were. She knew she needed to leave, and soon. "No. Just passing through. I'm leaving now," she said as she walked around the car, closing the doors and trunk.

"Whew. You smell that, Wilbur?" Beau asked.

"Oh yeah, brother, something's dead in that car, or there was something dead in there," Wilbur said and leaned on the driver's door preventing the contract killer from getting inside.

Charlie looked inside the luxury car at her purse, which had her gun inside it. She then looked at the shotgun Wilbur held. She knew she needed to make a move if she were to have the upper hand. *Two more bodies in the river*, she thought and grabbed Wilbur's gun. He wasn't ready for the move, or the one that followed. The shotgun blast sent Wilbur over the hood.

Beau lifted his own shotgun when he saw the woman turning around to face him.

Charlie quickly pulled the slide action back on the gun to chamber another round, but it was empty.

Beau stepped forward with his shotgun, raised it to his shoulder, and pointed it at the woman's head. "Bitch!"

The shot echoed through the woods and down the river.

Brian and Shelby walked down the beach, running into the water with the tide going out and then hurrying back when a large wave approached. They laughed and played like children on vacation. At some point during their frolicking, Shelby grabbed Brian's arm, which eventually led to them holding hands. As the sun dipped closer and closer to the Gulf, the two stood closer to each other.

Shelby shivered. "It's getting cooler."

Brian put his arm around her. "Come closer," he whispered.

Shelby put her arm around Brian's waist and moved into him. He looked down, into her green eyes. She was mesmerizing. Brian moved her long blonde hair out from her face. He pulled her closer and kissed her softly.

CHAPTER 9
DATE NIGHT

Brian walked Shelby back to the old blue house a little before six o'clock. Shelby told Brian about the problem she was having with her shower, and he agreed to look at it. When they walked inside, Brian stood in the living room and looked around for what all needed repair or improvements. His face said everything. He walked around the room, looking at the walls closely. He picked up a glass bottle from the windowsill and twisted it back and forth in his hand.

Shelby did not remember putting the bottle there. She didn't even remember removing it from the doorknob when she had rushed out earlier. *Odd*, she thought.

"It needs some work," Brian said as he placed the bottle back.

"It's bad, isn't it?" Shelby dismissed the bottle as a lapse in memory from rushing out to make sure Brian was all right.

"It's not too bad. It just needs some TLC. The walls are concrete and can be painted. The floor is covered in carpet and tile, both of which can be replaced. The ceiling leaked at one time, and I'm guessing it can use some new TPO."

"TPO?" Shelby asked.

"Yeah, it's a type of thermoplastic that goes on flat roofs."

"Oh."

Brian laughed. "Where's the bathroom?"

"Down the hall on the left," Shelby said and pointed.

Brian walked down the hall with Shelby right behind him. He spent a few minutes looking at the faucet and the knobs. He then sat on the toilet and looked at the sink. He turned the knobs, and both the hot and cold water came on. "Hmm."

"Hmm, what?" Shelby asked.

"I don't know."

Shelby raised an eyebrow. "I thought you built custom homes."

"I do. This isn't a custom home, and I don't do the plumbing myself. I hire most of the work out to other trade professionals. I run the project, sending bids out and making sure things get done on time," Brian explained.

"So you have no idea what's wrong with it?"

"Actually, I do. Somewhere, the water line going to the shower has been capped."

Shelby looked at the man with a blank expression. "Why would it be capped?"

"I don't know. I can look at it tomorrow, maybe follow the line from outside back into the house and see what's going on."

Shelby's shoulders dropped. "Tomorrow?"

"Yeah, why?"

"I really wanted to take a shower."

"I got a shower."

Hal and Rob were sitting in the Red Fish Restaurant's bar section, eating an early dinner. While they enjoyed raw oysters and boiled shrimp, Hal thought over a few things that had been bothering him. He thought maybe he needed more help, other than two convicts he wasn't familiar with.

"Rob, the sniper you hired in the desert to cover us when we met with Willy at the camper, is he available?"

"You mean the guy Jack hired. I don't know, but I can call him again. After he took care of the old guys by the creek bed, he kind of disappeared," Rob answered with a mouthful of bread.

Hal narrowed his eyes and pursed his lips. "You never met him?"

"No. Jack knew him and hired him. I got his number out of Jack's phone after he died."

"How'd Jack know him?"

"He was an inmate."

"Do you know his name?"

"No. Jack called him Smooth."

"Smooth?"

"Yep."

Evelyn looked out the window at the young woman who had moved into the old blue beach house across the street. She watched as Shelby made her way to the house next door, carrying her suitcase. Evelyn had met Shelby when she first arrived, and Evelyn hadn't been very nice to her, but it wasn't the time or place to make introductions. She really didn't need to talk to her about anything. She just wanted to see Shelby up close.

"What are you looking at?" Evelyn's "husband" asked.

"I'm just watching her."

"What's she doing now?"

Evelyn didn't answer. She just watched her and smiled.

"What's she doing?" He asked again.

Evelyn walked away from the window. "She's going over to his place, carrying her suitcase."

"What!" the man yelled as he stood and hurried to the window. "What does she think she's doing?"

"I don't know, but she's gorgeous, and I think he's taken notice."

Brian walked Shelby upstairs, grabbed her fresh towels, and showed her where the bathroom was. He stood at the door, waiting in an uncomfortable silence. Shelby placed her makeup bag on the countertop and reached for the door.

"You want to eat somewhere nice?" Brian suggested, finally breaking the silence.

"That would be nice. Do you want to maybe make us dinner reservations?" Shelby asked.

Brian realized he was just staring at her. He was embarrassed. "Yeah, I'll go downstairs and call around. You go ahead, do whatever you need, and use whatever you need."

"Okay," Shelby said and then slowly shut the door.

"Um, I'm going downstairs," Brian said once more and walked away.

Shelby turned on the water, undressed, and stepped into the shower. It was invigorating. She let the warm water run down her face as she closed her eyes and thought about Brian. She thought he was good looking, strong, and confident. She also thought things between them may be moving too fast, but maybe fast was what she needed.

Brian rushed downstairs and called a bunch of nice restaurants but didn't have any luck getting a reservation on such short notice. He sat on the couch and looked up restaurants that weren't on the island. He was about to call one more when he got a phone call. He looked at the number.

"Yeah… Why are you yelling… I'm keeping her close… I know that's not part of the deal… Me coming out here wasn't part of the deal, but that changed too!" Brian yelled into the phone and abruptly ended the call. He paced back and forth in the living room, thinking about what he should do. He headed upstairs.

Shelby got out of the shower and dried off. The humidity had caused the mirror to fog up. She removed the towel and wiped the mirror off, but the moisture in the room was too much. She opened the side window and then walked to the door.

Brian was about to knock on the bathroom door when it suddenly opened. He couldn't move. He couldn't blink. All he could do was stare at the beautiful, naked woman in front of him.

Shelby was just as surprised, and she froze for a second. She quickly shut the door.

"I'm sorry," Brian called.

Shelby fell back against the door. "It's okay. Did you need something?"

"There's nothing available on the island. I thought about calling somewhere else off the island. What do you think?"

Shelby thought about it for a second and then it hit her. "Give me a second. I have an idea." Shelby grabbed her phone off the toilet and texted Stacie.

I need food and I have a guest. Can you get us in? Please, please, with banana pudding on top.

A few seconds went by before Stacie texted back.

Yeah, he better be good looking!

Shelby snickered with excitement. "I got us in somewhere," she said through the door.

"Where?"

"I'll tell you when I come out."

"Okay, I'll go back downstairs. Come down when you're ready."

Hal and Rob were still sitting at Red Fish Restaurant. Rob continued to fill up on shrimp while Hal sat there thinking. Some things didn't add up, like the sniper, the old men in the burned-out Suburban, Agent Brian Forbes, and Willy's daughter.

"This sniper guy, do you know why Jack chose him?"

"Yeah, he said he was an Army Ranger. He did some tours in Afghanistan as a sniper or something."

Hal leaned forward, wrinkling his nose. "How do you know he killed Willy and the others?"

"He called me and told me after it was done. The coroner compared the medical records to the bodies that were in the Suburban, and they checked out. It was the three old guys."

"I guess. How did you pay him for the hit?"

"I dropped it where he asked. I mean, he did cover our asses at the camper. If it weren't for him, we wouldn't have gotten the one money bag. We got what was owed, and it's because of him."

"Yeah, it was, wasn't it? We got what was owed," Hal said and sat back in his chair. "Are you done?"

"Yeah, why? We still have time before we meet the others. You want to go somewhere else?"

"I want to go back to my condo before we head over to get the car."

Brian and Shelby took his car to Captain John's Seafood on the Beach. The parking lot was almost full, but Brian found a spot in the back. He ran around to the other side of his car to open the door for Shelby. When Shelby got out, she put her hand behind Brian's head and kissed him passionately.

Brian smiled when she finally pulled away. "I hope they can't get us in."

Shelby laughed. "We'll get in. I got connections."

"You got connections?"

"Yeah, I got people."

"Okay, we'll see."

The two walked in, and the men in the restaurant each turned to look at the gorgeous woman wearing a silky red shirt with white shorts. Shelby also wore the white high heels that Kim had picked out for her in Amarillo. She felt pretty, and Brian was making sure she did too. When he saw the other men looking at her, he got a little jealous. He placed his hand around her waist and pulled her close to him.

Stacie saw Shelby walk in and smiled at her. She then saw the man she was with, and her smile grew. She gave her a thumbs-up and rushed over to greet her and her date. "I have a table right over here for the two of you."

The couple followed the bartender to a table and sat down. Stacie stood by for a second, waiting for them to get comfortable.

"Here's our menu. Our special tonight is red snapper over rice pilaf. Can I start you two off with something to drink?" Stacie said as she handed both a menu.

"A white wine would be nice," Brian answered.

"Great. Do you need time to look at the menu?" Stacie asked.

"I think I'll have the shrimp and grits," Shelby said and looked across the table at her date.

"I'll have…"

"The shrimp and grits as well," Stacie stated before Brian could finish.

"How'd you know what I wanted?"

"Because you ordered it the other night. I kept it in the refrigerator. I'll warm it up and bring it right out to you," Stacie joked and hurried away.

Brian looked back at Shelby, who was laughing. "I guess she's one of your people, huh?"

"Yeah, she is."

"You don't think she really has my dinner from the other night, do you?"

"I don't know but probably not." Shelby answered and then started laughing again.

Brian shook his head and laughed along with her. "We're swapping plates when the food arrives!"

"Oh, no!"

When Hal got back to his place, he took out his laptop. He had a suspicion, and he needed to check it out. Rob took a seat and kept quiet as his boss waited for his computer to turn on.

"What are we doing here? What are you looking for?" Rob asked.

Hal logged into the prison database again. "I want to check on something."

"What?"

"Give me a minute. Now, what was that sniper's nickname?"

Rob scowled and pursed his lips. "Smooth. Why?"

Hal didn't answer. He typed the name Smooth into the alias box on the screen and pressed the enter key.

Rob leaned forward and propped himself on his elbows on the table. "Are you going to talk to me?"

Hal didn't answer. He kept his eyes on the screen until Smooth's picture appeared. "You gotta be kidding me."

"What?" Rob asked.

"It's Agent Brian Forbes," Hal said and turned the computer so Rob could see it.

"That's the guy next door. He's the one who stopped Charlie and me last night," Rob said and hit his fist on the table.

"We got a problem, but it could be all for the best. I need to call José and Mateo."

Shelby and Brian laughed throughout dinner, and they laughed some more over dessert. This time, Shelby shared the banana pudding with her dinner date. It was nearly eight o'clock when they ordered another bottle of wine. Shelby enjoyed spending the evening with Brian, and she liked how he made sure that she was the center of attention.

"The old beach house is needing so much work. I hope I can manage it. When you go back home after your vacation is over, may I call you for some advice?" Shelby asked.

Brian smiled; he knew what she was beating around the bush about. "My schedule is wide open right now. I'm thinking about staying here a little longer. Maybe I could help you out for a bit."

Shelby put her head down so he wouldn't see her grinning with glee. After she collected herself, she looked back up at him. "Do I look that helpless?"

"No, I think you'll be all right no matter if I help you or not."

Shelby was listening to Brian when suddenly her head felt heavy, and her eyes blinked rapidly. She dropped her spoon on the plate and grasped the table. Then Shelby was back in the box truck. Images of the kidnapper and the man who had saved her came rushing at her.

"Shelby, are you okay?" Brian jumped from his chair and caught her before she fell to the floor.

Stacie rushed over and stood on the other side of her. "What happened?"

"I don't know. She was fine one minute and then she turned pale and almost toppled over," Brian said as he held her in his arms.

Shelby heard the two of them talking. She was no longer in Albuquerque; she was back in the restaurant. "I'm okay. I don't know what happened. I just kind of lost myself for a minute."

"Maybe we should call an ambulance," Stacie said.

"No, I'm okay. It's probably just the wine."

"Are you sure? You've been through a lot lately," Brian said.

"I'm sure. Can you take me home?"

Brian looked up at Stacie and shrugged his shoulders. "Yeah, absolutely."

Brian paid for their food and left the restaurant after Stacie made him give her his phone number. The concerned bartender also took a picture of him. It made him laugh, but he understood why she was so careful. He was a stranger, after all.

When they got back to the beach house, he helped her onto the couch and sat next to her.

"How do you feel?" he asked.

Shelby looked up at him. "Better now."

"What happened back there?"

Shelby looked away.

Brian gently placed his hand on her chin and turned her face back toward his. "Tell me, please."

Shelby looked into his eyes and felt the need to tell him everything. Over the next thirty minutes, Shelby detailed the events that had brought her to Pensacola Beach. Brian listened without interrupting her, even though he already knew most of what she was telling him.

"So now, since the attack in Albuquerque, I've had these glimpses or flashbacks. I keep seeing this guy carrying me away. I'm sure he's the one I saw in the box truck fighting the guy who grabbed me. Sometimes I feel that if I close my eyes, I'll see him standing there. And—"

"And, you probably have a concussion. I think we should take you back to the hospital tomorrow and have them do a scan or something," Brian suggested, before she had any more memories come back.

Shelby tossed her hands into the air. "I don't know; maybe I should."

Brian looked into her eyes once again. He ran his hand down her neck and placed his other hand on the nape of her neck. He slowly pulled her close and kissed her gently.

Shelby pulled away and looked deeply into his eyes. "Slowly, okay," she whispered.

"Whatever you want," Brian whispered back. He then stood and picked her up.

She placed her arms around his neck and kissed him once more. He carried her up the stairs to the bedroom and laid her on the bed. He kissed her again and then removed his shirt and dropped it to the floor, revealing his muscular body.

Shelby slowly unbuttoned her top and slid out of it. She locked eyes with him as she unfastened her bra and laid it at the end of the bed. Brian admired her beautiful body for a moment before easing himself onto the bed. Shelby unbuttoned her shorts and slid them off. She wrapped her arms around his torso.

"Ouch!" Brian said when she bumped his wound with her arm.

Shelby quickly pulled back. "I'm sorry. We can stop."

Brian laughed. "Really, stop now? No, it's okay. I'll fight through the pain."

Shelby laughed too.

Hal had everything in place for when the couple returned. He stood at the window of Rob's beach house, keeping an eye outside. He looked at his watch. It was only a matter of time before he would have all the money. Soon, he would be on his way to someplace where no one knew who he was, but first, he needed to take care of some unfinished business.

"It'll all be over soon," Hal said as he looked at the Mustang sitting in the driveway across the street.

Chapter 10
Visions

Brian and Shelby lay in bed, wrapped in each other's arms. The night had been fantastic. Shelby had her reservations about getting involved with another man so soon after her breakup with Carter. Still, lying next to Brian, she couldn't imagine it being any other way. She could hear Brian steadily breathing and knew he was asleep. She slowly rolled away from him and crawled off the bed.

Shelby picked his shirt up and slid it over her head. She tiptoed across the bedroom to the bathroom. Once inside, she eased the door closed and turned on the light. Shelby stood in front of the mirror and looked at herself. "Shelby, Shelby, Shelby, what are you doing?" she asked herself. She turned the faucet on, splashed her face with cool water, and looked for a towel to dry off.

"Damn!" she whispered when she found the towel rack empty. Shelby opened the cabinet doors but couldn't locate something to dry her face. She then looked at the corner and saw a pile of towels. *How many towels can one man use?* she thought as she shook the water off her hands. When she was about to turn off the bathroom light, she saw something in the laundry pile that caught her eye.

Brian was awakened by a noise. He looked around the room but didn't see Shelby. He quickly scooted off the bed, opened the nightstand drawer, and pulled out his .45. Brian stayed low and surveyed his surroundings, and he saw the light glowing from underneath the bathroom door. He took a breath, believing the noise he'd heard was Shelby going to the bathroom. He slowly stood and didn't move for a second.

Then he heard something or someone downstairs. Brian slid his pants on, looked at the bathroom door, and decided to go downstairs to see what or who was there.

Shelby slowly walked over, stood over the pile of dirty clothes, and stared at what looked like a white hoodie. She bent down and pulled the garment out of the pile. The letters UNLV were clearly visible on the front, along with bloodstains that covered a large portion of the hoodie. Shelby dropped to her knees, and without warning, she was back in the box truck.

She felt the man's hands on her. She then saw him standing there, smoking a cigarette. Shelby tried to recall more, but there was nothing except the sounds of the two men scuffling and then it stopped. A moment later Shelby felt someone carrying her.

Shelby opened her eyes, and she was back in the bathroom. "No, no, I need to know," Shelby cried. She took a deep breath, held the hoodie close to her, and closed her eyes.

Brian walked down the stairs with his .45 at the ready. He stayed in the shadows to conceal his approach. When he reached the landing at the bottom, he heard someone moving around in the kitchen. He paused for a moment and surveyed the darkness around him. He then slowly moved toward the kitchen.

Shelby tried to take herself back to Albuquerque, but she couldn't stop crying. "Stop it! Concentrate," she told herself, and again she closed her eyes and imagined being carried by the man in the hoodie. She already knew who it was, but she needed to see it. She needed to see him.

Once more, she was back there, in his arms. Again, she heard him say, "You'll be all right," and he started to look down at her.

Brian walked into the kitchen, slowly opened the swinging door, and found nothing but a bright flash of light.

Shelby kept her eyes fixated on the man carrying her. As the two entered the light of the convenience store, she finally saw him.

She opened her eyes just as the sound of a gunshot rang out. "Brian!" She shouted and ran out of the bathroom, down the stairs, and into the kitchen.

"Nice of you to join us," Hal said as he walked around the large granite counter.

Shelby looked at Brian, who was lying on the floor as his blood pooled around him. She dropped to her knees and put her hand on his back. "Who are you?" she yelled as she looked around the kitchen at the people standing there.

"Grab her!" Hal yelled to José and Mateo.

The two brothers grabbed her by the arms and lifted her.

"What do you want with me?"

Rob stepped forward and gripped Shelby by her face. "We want to know what your father left you in that envelope, and we want the car."

"It's all next door," Shelby admitted.

"Then let's go get it," Hal said.

The two brothers escorted Shelby out the door and into the yard, with Hal and Rob following close behind them.

When they were between the two houses, Rob stopped and grabbed Hal by the arm. "Wait. Where's Charlie?"

Hal looked around and didn't see Charlie anywhere. Charlie had not called or answered Hal's text earlier, but the warden thought his contract killer would have still shown up, knowing what was at stake.

"Stop!" Hal ordered José and Mateo.

Both men stopped and looked back at their employer. "What's wrong?" José asked.

Hal suspiciously looked around. "Something's not right." He looked to his right and saw someone moving out from behind the old blue beach house. He squinted his eyes to try to see who it was.

"I gave you a lot of money, but it wasn't enough, was it? You had to have it all, didn't you? Greed, it's a compelling thing."

"Yes, it is, Willy," Hal said.

"What?" Rob asked and stepped forward for a better look. "You were right. He's alive."

"Yeah, he set it all up. He had his old cellmate Smooth run interference for him. Jay worked in the infirmary and changed their medical records. Then he arranged to have Jack hire Smooth to cover us in the desert, but he wasn't covering us, was he, Willy?"

"No, Brian Suthers or 'Smooth' as we call him was covering us, and he did a good job of it too. By the way, Hal, how's the leg?"

Hal chuckled sarcastically. "Funny."

"Dad, is that really you?" Shelby asked.

Hal stepped closer to her and placed his gun at her head. "C'mon on out, where we can see you better—nice and slow, like with your hands in the air."

Willy did as he was ordered and kept his eye on the man holding a gun to his daughter's head. He glanced to his left and saw the one thing he needed. He started walking toward Hal.

"That's far enough," Hal ordered.

Willy didn't listen. He kept walking forward.

"Stop!" Hal ordered.

Willy didn't hesitate.

"Stop!" Hal yelled once more and aimed his gun at the elderly man.

"Now!" Willy yelled and then dropped to the sand just as a bullet whizzed by.

Mateo didn't know what hit him. The .308 round entered his skull right between the eyes. He dropped to his knees and fell forward into the island beach sand. Hal ran to his right and found cover behind one of the piers supporting the beach house.

A wounded Brian looked over the scope of his rifle at Shelby. "Run to me!" he yelled.

José ran for cover and yelled something in Spanish. Then two of his associates came running out of the shadows, firing wildly in Shelby's and Willy's directions. Willy rolled to his left and looked up at Shelby, who was frozen with fear. Bullets hit the ground around her.

"Smooth, cover me," Willy ordered as he got up and ran to his daughter.

Brian got to his knees and fired at the two men who'd appeared out of the shadows. He caught the one on his right with a bullet to his chest. The other man found cover behind a small sand dune.

Rob was still in shock, hiding in the street behind a car. He didn't know what to do, but when he saw Willy running for his daughter, he carefully aimed his pistol at him.

"Robby, how are things?"

Rob turned around and found Roscoe standing there, holding a 9 mm on him.

"Don't even think about it!"

Rob didn't listen. He raised his gun and quickly fired his weapon. Roscoe was faster, and he placed two bullets into the man's chest. The round Rob fired ricocheted off the road and caught Roscoe in the shoulder, which sent him running behind another car for cover.

José dropped down and hid behind one of the support piers under Rob's rented beach house across the street. He saw his brother go down, and it drove him to get to the man who had killed him. He peered through the darkness and saw the man Hal had shot in the kitchen of the beach house taking cover on the deck. He looked hurt, but he wasn't dead, but he soon would be if José could get to him.

When Willy got to Shelby, he grabbed her by the arms and pulled her toward Brian's beach house. At the stairs, she started to struggle.

"I thought you were dead!" she yelled and pulled away from his grasp.

"Not now, sweetheart," Willy ordered and grabbed at her again.

Shelby pulled away once more, just as a bullet found Willy's right leg, fired from Hal's gun. The elderly man dropped to the ground while Shelby screamed and knelt over him.

"How's that feel, Willy? Just returning the favor!" Hal called as he slowly moved from one pier support to the next, getting closer to his intended target.

Brian heard Shelby screaming. He got up to run. Bullets whizzed by him, then one found its way into his arm. Brian fell back on the deck with a gunshot wound to his arm to go with the one he already had in his chest. He knew the direction the bullet came from, but he couldn't stand without getting hit again. "Shit," he mumbled.

"Cover me!" José ordered his other man as he walked down the side of the beach house to the back deck. The other man stood and directed the barrel of his pistol at the back deck as José made his approach.

José got ready to surprise the man who had killed his brother.

"Now, Smooth!" Jay yelled as he opened fire with his Thompson submachine gun on José's cover man, killing him before he knew what happened.

José spun around toward the shooting.

Brian heard Jay's command, and with everything, he sat up and found José standing there at the edge of the deck. He aimed his gun at José's head. "Psst."

José quickly turned his gun back toward the man on the deck. Brian pulled the trigger, and José fell backward onto the sand.

Shelby was treating Willy's leg when Hal walked up behind them. He placed the gun barrel against Shelby's head. "Don't move."

Shelby froze in place and gazed at her father. "Please stop!"

"As long as I get the money, you'll live," Hal said with a smile.

"What's going on over there?" the elderly woman from across the street yelled from her porch.

Hal looked up, and that was all it took. He never heard the shot, but he did feel the bullet from Brian's .308 as it ripped through his heart. The warden dropped his gun and fell to the ground. Police sirens wailed in the distance. Brian dropped the rifle and collapsed.

Suddenly, a black SUV pulled up with Jay and Roscoe inside. "We gotta get out of here!" Jay yelled as he ran around the front of the vehicle to help Willy get inside.

"Get Smooth and place the bags of cocaine in his place," Willy ordered after Jay eased him into the back seat.

Jay took off toward the beach house to help the younger man.

Shelby stood next to her father. She was in shock.

Willy reached out and took her by the hand. "Everything will be okay."

"What's going on? What do I do now?" Shelby asked.

"Nothing. You know nothing. Now, go over to Evelyn's place. You were over there when this gang war happened."

"I don't understand," Shelby stated as she watched Brian being placed into the back seat, next to her father. He was still conscious, but he looked terrible. Shelby ran to the other side and grabbed his hand.

Brian opened his eyes and looked at her. "I'll see you soon," he said in a soft whisper.

Jay pulled Shelby away from the vehicle and passed her off to Evelyn. The two women stood there and watched as the SUV sped away.

"Come on, honey," Evelyn said as she put her arm around Shelby and pulled her toward her beach house.

It had been six months since that night, and Shelby had not heard from her father or Brian since. She and Evelyn had talked to the police when they arrived. As far as the police were concerned, the two women had been out all evening and had not seen anything until they saw all the emergency vehicles on their street. Evelyn did most of the talking while Shelby agreed with what the elderly woman told them. Willy had made all the arrangements, and he was selling the entire incident as a drug deal gone bad.

Shelby learned that Evelyn was Jay's younger sister and, to Shelby's surprise, her father's girlfriend. Apparently, Willy and the others had planned on leaving the United States after they faked their deaths in Las Vegas, but Warden Baker had other plans for them.

It started out as a simple plan to get Shelby safely out of Las Vegas after the camper ordeal, but it had turned into a huge fiasco.

Evelyn told Shelby how her father had snuck into the old beach house and checked on her as she slept one night. Willy had come back to Evelyn's place that night beaming with pride when he found the bottle sitting on the doorknob. He had boasted to Evelyn that his daughter was using a trick he had taught her. Willy had made a promise to himself that he would show Shelby how to beat the bottle on the doorknob if she'd ever let him.

Shelby sat in Evelyn's beach house, watching the evening news. The two had had a late evening of dinner and drinks with Shelby's friends, Stacie and Kim. Kim had come in from Amarillo for a visit. Shelby and Evelyn had plans of spending the next day at the beach with them both. As the two women were making plans, the local news came on. Suddenly, they stopped what they were doing to listen to the reporter on the television. An image of Brian's rented beach house filled the screen. Shelby picked up the remote and turned the volume up.

"The Escambia County Sheriff's Office has concluded its investigation into the shooting that took place at the beach house right behind me six months ago," the news reporter stated.

Shelby and Evelyn watched and moved closer to the screen when Warden Henry Baker's image appeared next.

"It has been determined that Nevada State Prison Warden Henry Baker had come to Pensacola Beach to sell cocaine to a local drug gang when the shooting occurred. Since the shooting, the police have connected inmates and local gang members to some of the Nevada Prison System employees. The sheriff's office is working closely with the Nevada Department of Corrections to determine who is involved and who may still be involved. An anonymous source identified Warden Henry Baker as the ringleader of this multi-state drug ring. The warden was one of the people killed here, along with one of his prison guards. In the end, we may never know exactly what occurred here on Maldonado Drive. I'm Heather Shields, Channel Six News, live at Pensacola Beach."

Evelyn turned and looked at Shelby. "We should get ready to leave after this weekend."

Shelby looked at Evelyn. "You think so?"

Evelyn smiled at the young woman. "Yes, I do. I think we need a vacation."

Shelby beamed. "Where?"

EPILOGUE
VACATION

The sun was already setting by the time Shelby and Evelyn made it to Costa Rica. The car that met them at the airport was driven by a very nice man. He offered the ladies cold water bottles that he had chilling inside the plastic cooler next to him, in the passenger seat. Shelby was not accustomed to traveling to such exotic places. When she learned of their vacation destination, she downloaded a Spanish-speaking app and began learning the language.

Shelby had two concerns, and her thoughts shifted from one to the other during the flight from Miami to Costa Rica. First, she wondered if she and Brian would be able to start where they had left off. Second, she didn't know how her relationship with her father would be. She still had mixed emotions about her feelings for him. Over the past six months, with Evelyn, she had developed more of an understanding about her father. It included his life and who he was as a man, friend, and husband to her mother.

Now, it was up to Shelby to decide what kind of father he was. As the driver took them closer to their destination, Shelby pulled the envelope that had been given to her months ago in

Las Vegas from her purse. She looked to Evelyn, who scooted closer and placed her arm around the young woman. Shelby opened the envelope for the first time and took out an old, wrinkled sheet of paper. She carefully opened it up, and a single tear dropped from the corner of her eye as she looked at the crayon drawing of her family in front of the beach house. After a moment, she smiled and decided that she was willing to try to work things out if he was.

When the car pulled up to the house on the beach, Shelby saw Willy, Roscoe, and Jay standing there in the driveway, waiting for them. Behind the three men on the porch was a taller man. He was wearing a white cotton long-sleeve, button-down shirt, blue board shorts, and white deck shoes. Shelby recognized Brian right away. He was smiling, which to her was a good sign. As the car came to a stop, Brian rushed over and opened the door for her. Shelby jumped out and threw her arms around his neck. He kissed her deeply and passionately.

Willy and the others just watched the young couple. "How are you going to deal with that?" Jay asked, at which he and Roscoe laughed aloud.

Willy looked at Jay with a grin on his face. "I guess the same way you have to deal with this," Willy replied as he walked toward Evelyn, took her into his arms, and kissed her.

"That's not right!" Roscoe declared and laughed even louder.

Shelby looked at the two men. "What's so funny?" she asked.

Willy smiled at his two friends and then turned toward his daughter. He held his arms out. Shelby looked at him for a second and stepped into his arms.

"Hi, Daddy."

About the Author

Michael grew up in Pensacola, Florida, where he spent the summer months as a youth at the beach, tubing down the river or splashing around in a pool near his grandmother's home. After graduating from high school, he joined the US Army and served in the Military Police Corps. After nearly seven and a half years, Michael left the military. He took a position at the Colorado Springs Police Department, where he served the community for ten years. An injury on duty forced him into early retirement from policing. Currently, Michael is the Department Chair of the Criminal Justice Department at a local community college. Michael earned a Bachelor of Science in Sociology with an emphasis in Criminology from Colorado State University and a Master of Criminal Justice from the University of Colorado.

Michael started his writing career as a ghostwriter for a publisher of textbooks. Eventually, he co-authored a textbook. Michael has always had the desire to write fiction. Through the encouragement of his family and friends, Michael started writing mystery fiction and hasn't stopped. Michael's wife, Stefanie, still catches him daydreaming as he drives down the highway thinking about different stories. The facial expressions that he makes reveal to her that somewhere in his mind, he's reviewing a chapter, scene, or dialogue between characters for a new book.